D0372008

NO LONGER PROPERTY OF
SEATTLE PUBLIC LIBRARY

RECEIVED
JAN 11 2023
By_____

HORACE
&
BUNWINKLE
THE CASE OF THE FISHY FAIRE

Also available by PJ Gardner

Horace & Bunwinkle
Horace & Bunwinkle: The Case of the Rascally
Raccoon

PJ GARDNER

HORACE & BUNWINKLE

THE CASE OF THE FISHY FAIRE

ILLUSTRATIONS BY
DAVID MOTTRAM

BALZER + BRAY
An Imprint of HarperCollinsPublishers

Balzer + Bray is an imprint of HarperCollins Publishers.

Horace & Bunwinkle: The Case of the Fishy Faire
Text copyright © 2022 by PJ Switzer
Illustrations copyright © 2022 by David Mottram
All rights reserved. Printed in the United States of America.
No part of this book may be used or reproduced in any manner
whatsoever without written permission except in the case of brief
quotations embodied in critical articles and reviews. For information
address HarperCollins Children's Books, a division of HarperCollins
Publishers, 195 Broadway, New York, NY 10007.
www.harpercollinschildrens.com

Library of Congress Control Number: 2022933997
ISBN 978-0-06-294660-7

Typography by Kathy H. Lam
22 23 24 25 26   PC/LSCH   10 9 8 7 6 5 4 3 2 1

First Edition

To Neil, the best support a writer could ask for and the funniest gag writer I know. None of this would be possible without you.

HORACE
&
BUNWINKLE
THE CASE OF THE FISHY FAIRE

1

The Green-Eyed Monster

For Horace Homer Higgins III, the Renaissance couldn't end soon enough. It was so loud, not to mention dirty and terribly dangerous. There was a man wandering around breathing fire and another who claimed to be a sheriff but tried to duel anyone with a sword. Which was a lot of people. Apparently, waving a sword around and flashing daggers were common in Merrie Olde England.

It was a full-time job keeping his human, Eleanor, safe.

And then there was the smell—*smells*, really. Human sweat, animal dung, and grease from the different food stalls next to them, all mixed together into a disgusting stench.

When this Renaissance Faire ended and life was back to normal, Horace was going to sleep for a week.

"I wish we could live here forever!" Bunwinkle flopped down next to him.

"We don't live here now. We just visit. Besides, it will be over in a few weeks."

Hopefully.

Bunwinkle smacked her lips. "Weh, I wuv it hewr."

"What are you eating now?" Horace asked with a sigh.

"Nuffin'." His piglet sister gulped loudly, then turned to him. "See?" She opened her mouth wide.

"It was a churro, wasn't it?"

Her eyes grew round. "How did you know?"

He leaned over and licked the side of her face. "You're covered in cinnamon and sugar."

"Dang it! I'll just have to clean off the rest myself." She stretched out her tongue and cleared a spot on her cheek.

"That's not going to do any good unless your tongue can reach behind your ears." He brushed a clump of the sweet mixture from her neck. "Good heavens! How did you make such a mess of yourself?"

"My head got stuck in the treat stand."

Horace frowned. "What treat stand?"

"The one behind the churro cart."

He thought for a moment. There wasn't anything behind that cart except a compost bin. "Bunwinkle! That stand isn't for treats, it's for garbage."

Wonderful. Was he going to have to follow her around to keep her safe as well? But that would mean leaving Eleanor unprotected. What was a dog to do?

"What are you two discussing so seriously?"

The voice belonged to Dean Royal, alpaca farmer and general nuisance. He stood over them, holding a tray of drinks and smiling. His dark hair had been gelled and styled and he was wearing new jeans. Horace could tell from the smell.

Dean was the one who had arranged for the Renaissance Faire to take place in the field behind the Homestead. Before that Eleanor had been struggling to pay bills, but Dean had saved the day. Of course, Horace would have figured out how to help her eventually.

Then the human nuisance had encouraged Eleanor and her friend Clary to run an old-fashioned ice-cream stand at the faire, the kind where people made their own ice cream in a bucket. Eleanor had jumped at the chance. Her attempts to make cheese out of the milk she got from the goats on the Homestead had all failed. But the ice cream business was doing well.

Except for the fact that Dean "dropped by" five times a day and distracted Eleanor from her responsibilities.

Dean leaned down and wiped some cinnamon and sugar from Bunwinkle's head. "You've got to stay out of the compost, or El is going to have a fit. If you want a yummy treat, you come to me. Okay, sweet thing?"

All Bunwinkle's white spots turned pink and she giggled. "Isn't Dean the best?"

"No," Horace grumbled.

"Wow. Jealous much?"

He ignored her, focusing instead on Dean as he walked over to Eleanor.

It was the ingratitude that bothered Horace the most. He watched over Eleanor and Bunwinkle day and night, kept them safe from ducks and other dangerous creatures. In fact, just two weeks ago he'd saved the Homestead from an unscrupulous dairy mogul. Bunwinkle had helped a little with that one, but the point was Eleanor had *him*. She didn't need anyone else.

"Hello, ladies. I brought you coffee."

Eleanor's face lit up when Dean set the cup on the table in front of her. "How did you know?" She took a big drink. "You're the best!"

Bunwinkle nudged Horace with her shoulder. "See, even Ellie thinks so."

That was only because Eleanor had been blinded by all the nice things the man had done. She couldn't see him clearly like Horace did. Dean was up to something. Horace didn't know what yet, but he would find out.

"Can I help with anything?" Dean asked.

"Yes!" both women said at the same time.

Clary handed him a pair of plastic gloves. "We

need to separate the fruit into individual serv-
ings."

Dean put on the gloves and sat down next to
Eleanor.

Hmph! That was far too close.

Horace waited for Eleanor to say something or
at the very least move away from the nuisance,
but she simply smiled and handed Dean a con-
tainer of blueberries.

This would not do. Horace would have to take
matters into his own paws. He stood and then
calmly marched over to where Dean and Eleanor
sat. There was just enough room between them to
fit Horace's head. This was going to be easier than
he'd thought.

He quietly stuck his head in the gap. A quick
lick on the back of the arm made Dean jump,
which gave Horace space to hop up. All in all, it
had taken less than thirty seconds to secure his
place on the bench.

Almost immediately a cold, wet snout pressed
against Horace's back.

"Hey, make room for me." Bunwinkle squirmed
up next to him.

Irritation rolled over Horace. "No, this isn't a job for little sisters."

Bunwinkle snorted. "What job? Eating all the fruit?"

"Sorry, guys, you can't be near the food," Eleanor said, nudging them off the bench with her elbow.

Dean smiled at them, then tossed a couple of strawberries their way. Bunwinkle jumped and caught them both in her mouth.

"Mmm, eese are dewicious!"

Hmph.

While the humans laughed, a woman wearing a shower cap and a fancy yellow dress rushed into the stall. It was Eleanor's friend Jennie. She was one of Horace's favorite people, not just because she shared his love of french fries, but also because she always seemed to know how he was feeling.

"They're back!" Jennie shouted, waving her phone around. "They're back!"

"Who's back?" Eleanor asked.

Jennie scooped Horace up, then squeezed in between Eleanor and Dean on the bench. "The Horse Apple Gang. I've done several podcasts about them. Remember?"

"Hey!" Bunwinkle snorted. "Me too."

"Sorry, Winkie." Jennie reached back and lifted Horace's sister onto her lap, her shower cap falling off her long black hair in the process. "Shoot, my hair's going to dry before I can set it." She waved her hand. "But it doesn't matter. Not when the gang is back."

Eleanor nodded then turned to Dean and Clary, who wore matching confused expressions. "Jennie's a bit of a true crime buff. She does a podcast all about real-life cases. She read a *lot* of Nancy Drew books when we were kids."

"Nice. Did I make fun of you when you bought a house in the country so you could live out your 'Little House on the Prairie' dreams?"

"You sang 'Old McHiggins's Farm' to me for a solid month before I moved."

"Oh yeah." Jennie laughed. "Anyway, back to the Horse Apple Gang. Last week they robbed another house—and it was in *this* area."

Bunwinkle leaned close to Horace and whispered, "What's a horse apple? Is it just a really big piece of fruit?"

Horace sighed again. "It's a figure of speech. The apple in question is actually dung."

"Yuck. I would definitely not eat that."

He sighed heavier this time. "Could you please be quiet? I'm trying to listen to Jennie's story."

When they caught up with the conversation, Jennie had laid her phone down on the table and was scrolling through what looked like notes.

"The gang got their name because they use horses for their getaway. The droppings are the only clues they leave."

Clary frowned. "Wouldn't horses stand out in the city?"

"They only rob estates and mansions in remote areas, and they're very specific about what they take. Cash, silver, high-value items that are easy to carry. Like, at this last job at Mildred Hewel's country house, they took a bunch of precious gems and jewelry. They probably would have stolen more if she hadn't come home and caught them."

As she talked, Jennie opened a bag of strawberries and started eating them. Every fourth one she'd feed to Horace or Bunwinkle. She really was a delightful human.

Eleanor didn't seem to agree, though.

"Jennifer Andrea Pike, if you eat another strawberry I'm going to take a picture of you in that hideous yellow dress and share it with your students."

"Go ahead. Everyone at the school already knows about it. I'm posting tons of pictures on my social media. I'm determined to win the school's 'Most Interesting Summer Vacation' prize this year. Nothing is going to beat playing the queen in a Renaissance Faire." Jennie quickly split the last strawberry in two and fed the pieces to Horace and Bunwinkle. "It really is a hideous dress, though. The hem is so uneven I keep tripping on it. And the bodice is lumpy—it's like it's filled with rocks. I think I'm going to take it home tonight and fix it up."

At that moment several of the faire actors walked by.

A round man in a red costume stopped suddenly and did a fancy bow. "My queen, what brings you here?" His gray beard and mustache moved as he spoke, as though they weren't attached to his face.

"Oh, man, he's wearing a fake beard." Bunwinkle giggled.

Jennie hopped to her feet, then curtsied. "Apologies, my liege, I was led astray by an offering of strawberries."

The king stared at Jennie with an odd expression on his face. "My dear, what on earth are you wearing? That's not the queen's dress."

"It didn't fit, so they gave me this one," Jennie said, ending the game they were playing. "It's terrible, isn't it? I'm going to fix up a different one at Ellie's house tonight."

"Oh yes. That's probably for the best." He looked relieved. "I'd hate for us to clash. And now we must return to our dressing rooms before the faire opens."

"Bye, everyone." Jennie took the king's arm and waved at them.

"Well, I have to get going too." Dean stood from

the table. "I've got to get the alpacas fed."

Horace shook his head. Jennie's visit had distracted him from the Dean situation. He had to focus on the problem at hand.

Dean stepped closer to Eleanor, his arms slightly raised as though he wanted a hug. Horace leaped up and growled for all he was worth. There would be no hugging on his watch. Dean glanced over his shoulder at Horace, then back at Eleanor.

"I guess I'll see you later," he said.

Clary waved. "Stay out of trouble."

"Can't make any promises." He winked at Eleanor, then turned and walked up the lane.

There it was. The man couldn't even make a simple promise to behave! Rotten to the core, Horace knew it.

Wait a minute! Maybe he could catch Dean making mischief. If he had proof that Dean was up to no good, maybe Eleanor would send the man on his way.

While Eleanor and Clary were busy setting up buckets and getting ready for the faire to open for the day, Horace was going to do a little surveillance.

"I'm going to the privy. Don't follow me," he told Bunwinkle.

"Right," she snorted. "And I'm a purple bumblebee." She hopped to her feet and bumped his side. "Come on, before the gates open and it gets too crowded to tail him."

Sometimes Bunwinkle surprised him. Like now. She clearly liked Dean, but she'd agreed to help Horace track him anyway. Unless . . .

"Are you doing this so you can get more food?"

But she was already gone. "Sorry. Can't hear you. Too busy being a pet-tective."

He hurried after her. Well, whatever the reason, he was glad she was with him.

Four stalls over, Dean stopped to chat with the court jester, who was already wearing his ridiculous face paint and green costume. Bells had been sewn on so that he jingled and jangled everywhere he went. And he went *everywhere*, singing silly songs and playing the lute. It was all highly undignified.

Horace ducked inside the closest booth. He heard a few words of their conversation—fields, foot traffic—but that was all.

"Did you hear any of that?" Horace asked Bunwinkle.

"Uhn, uh."

"What?" He turned to find her eating corn on the cob. "Where did you get that?"

"Judy gave it to me."

"Who's Judy?"

"The corn on the cob lady," she said.

Why had he expected a serious answer?

He took a deep breath and refocused his attention on Dean, who was shaking the jester's hand. As soon as the jingling stopped, it was time to move again.

Dean waved and said hello to everyone they passed. Then he made a left turn at Cold Steel Avenue—where the swords and daggers were sold—but stopped almost immediately to talk to a tall, blond man with a serious expression. It was Ted, the man who owned and ran the faire.

Horace hid behind a sign advertising bodkins, whatever those were. This time he could hear everything. Apparently Ted just wanted to thank Dean for helping him haul in supplies. That didn't

help Horace at all. They shook hands and it was time to go again.

"You ready?" Horace asked.

"U beh."

Horace closed his eyes. Don't turn around. *Do not* turn around.

But he had to. Bunwinkle's snout was buried in a basket of fish and chips.

Horace couldn't believe it. "You . . . you had Paul's french fries and you didn't share?"

Her head hung down. He hoped it was from shame, but suspected it was so she could gobble up whatever was left in the basket.

"I'm sorry," she said when she finished chewing. "It's just that Paul called me over and said I looked hungry and I probably needed a full order to myself because I'm a growing girl."

"Paul said all that, did he?" Horace glared at her.

"Look, Dean's getting away!" she shouted, and ran after the human, a french fry stuck to the side of her face.

They would discuss this matter later.

From Cold Steel Avenue Dean continued on to Tournament Square.

"Where is he going?" Horace whispered. "His farm is the other way."

"Hey, it's Shoo!" Bunwinkle said excitedly. She pointed at a familiar figure scurrying behind a trash can, a small bag held in his paws.

Shoo the raccoon was a new friend of theirs.

During their last case, they'd saved him from animal control, and he'd saved them from a delinquent lemur. Shoo was also an oddball who could distract the most focused of animals. And they simply did not have time to be distracted right now.

Bunwinkle hopped up and down and shouted, "Sh—"

A horrible screech filled the air, cutting her off. The sound grated on Horace's eardrums and made his teeth ache. It was a noise only a monster could produce. Dread filled his heart. There was another screech, closer this time, and a shadow passed over them.

"Get down!" Horace shouted as he dropped to the ground.

2

Cry Fowl

Winkie squeezed her eyes shut and ducked down next to Horace.

"What is it?" she whispered.

It had to be something really bad for Horace to freak out like that. Something scary. Like maybe a dragon. Yeah, a fire-breathing one. That would be so cool. Dangerous but cool. She shivered. But it wasn't Horace's voice that answered.

"What ho, strangers. What seek ye at my faire?"

Hmm, that didn't sound like a dragon. Winkie peeked one eye open. A gigantic bird with brown and off-white feathers and some sharp-looking talons perched on the sign right above them.

Winkie recognized her. She was a part of the play the faire put on every day. They made a big deal of her flying in with messages for the king, and then at the end she was the one who pulled the mask off the villain. She got her own curtain call and everything.

"This is what you freaked out about?" Winkie turned to Horace. "It's just a bird."

Horace answered with a low, rumbly growl. He was on all fours again in his power pose—head up, chest out, teeth bared.

"You wound me, pig. I am no mere bird. I am a red-tailed hawk." She sounded exactly like the actors in the play, all fancy and stuff. "And the greatest living avian actress of my generation."

"Oh, sorry."

"Don't apologize to it," Horace snapped. "It will only see that as a sign of weakness. Get behind me. I'll protect you."

"What say you, knave?" the bird asked.

"Oh, his name's not Knave, it's Horace," Winkie said. "And I'm Winkie. Horace calls me by my full name, Bunwinkle. But I think that makes me sound super grown-up, like a teacher or a librarian."

Horace growled louder. "Don't tell it our names. Can't you see how dangerous it is?"

"You dare call me dangerous? Well, 'I scorn you, scurvy companion!'" She looked down at them. "That's from Shakespeare's *Henry IV, Part 2*, act 2, scene 4."

"Hmph." Horace turned his nose up at her. "Though I am sorely tempted, I will not insult you in response. 'It is better to take many Injuries than to give one.' That's from New Englander Benjamin

Franklin's *Poor Richard's Almanack*, 1735."

Winkie was totally lost. It's like they were talking in code.

While she was trying to work it out, a shadow moved over her, and someone breathed on her neck.

Please let it be a dragon.

It wasn't a dragon. It was just Smith and Jones, the two old horses from the Homestead. Only they didn't look like they usually did. Their coats were all shiny, and someone had braided their manes and put flower wreaths on their heads. They looked awesome!

Well, except for the dark circles under Jones's eyes and the drool running down Smith's chin.

"Is he asleep?" Winkie asked.

Jones looked over at his brother.

Smith muttered, "Told you it was a three-man job."

"Yeah, I reckon he's sleeping," Jones said.

"While he's walking around?" she asked.

Jones nodded. "While he's walking. While he's pulling a cart. Shoot, he slept through the trip to the North Pole the other night."

The North Pole?

Winkie looked over at her brother to see if he had heard that, but he was totally focused on the bird.

Horace growled loudly. "Good thing you're here. We could use some help removing this detestable creature from the area."

The hawk glared at Horace and scratched her talons on the sign.

"You be careful now, that's Uta Hawken." Jones gave the bird an uncomfortable nod. "She's got a reputation for scratching people. We heard all about her on the radio. Didn't we, Smith?"

"How was I supposed to know she was packing heat?" Smith mumbled.

"Those were false rumors. I never scratched anyone . . . who didn't deserve it." Uta puffed up her chest. "If this cur knows what's good for him, he'll behave, for I am the eyes and ears of this faire. I know everything that happens. One misstep and I'll . . ." She lifted her left foot and flexed her talons at them.

Winkie gulped. "Hey, Horace, maybe you shouldn't fight with her. She looks pretty tough."

"I'm not afraid of those talons or anything else about her," Horace sneered, never taking his eyes off the bird.

"What about the feathers?" Winkie whispered. "You hate feathers."

"Well—" A loud whistle interrupted Horace.

Uta tilted her head, then a second whistle came. "I must be off. I have important work to do for my human, Ted. You know him; he's the one who runs this faire." She sneered at Horace and Winkie. "Lackeys."

"Hey!"

That wasn't fair. Winkie had been nice and

polite. It wasn't her fault that birds turned Horace into dog-zilla. Most of the time he was pretty boring, talking about New England and stuff.

He watched the bird fly away, muttering something under his breath. Once she was out of sight, he turned to Winkie.

"We've got to get Eleanor away from this place. Between Dean and that foul creature, it's too difficult for me to keep her safe."

"Is Dean that young feller that Miss Eleanor is sweet on?" Jones asked.

That was the wrong thing to say. Horace's nose holes got real big and he pressed his lips together.

"She is *not* sweet on him."

The old gray horse looked at Winkie. She quickly shook her head and mouthed, "Drop it."

"Well, what would an old workhorse like me know about human romance?"

"Romance?" Horace muttered. "As if Eleanor would ever get romantic about someone like Dean."

Winkie waved her hoof to get Jones to move to a different topic.

Jones nodded and said, "You don't need to

worry about him anyway. We passed him as he was leaving the faire. Didn't we, brother?"

Smith snorted. "That's not what Otis Mayes said."

"Wait, who's Otis Mayes?" Winkie asked. Geez, sleep-talking Smith was even more confusing than awake-talking Jones.

"It doesn't matter where he went as long as he's not with Eleanor," her brother said.

Winkie sighed. Horace needed to get over this problem with Dean.

Horace was super quiet on the way back to the stall. He had the saddest expression on his face, like the one he got when Ellie was mad at him. Winkie didn't know how to make him feel better. Maybe she should see if Paul would give her some more food. French fries always put Horace in a good mood.

When they reached the Pickle on a Stick cart, Winkie stopped. She couldn't take the silence anymore.

"Hey, let's just talk about it. That's what you always tell me to do."

Horace stared at her as if she'd grown another snout. "New Englanders do not talk about their feelings. They master them."

"That doesn't sound very healthy to me."

"You're simply too young to understand." He lifted his chin and said in his snootiest voice, "Besides, I'm perfectly fine."

Except he wasn't. She could see that even if he couldn't.

When they got back, there was a crowd of people from the faire around the ice-cream tent. It didn't take long to find out why. In front of the tent was a guy wearing a bright red shirt and puffy pants dotted with heart shapes. He was making a huge ruckus.

Horace groaned. "Not the turnip man again."

The turnip man—also known as Titus—was the only thing Winkie didn't like about the faire. He had a small cart called the Merchant of Vegetables, which sounded great except he only sold boring vegetables like turnips and parsnips. He wouldn't even sell potatoes because he said they weren't grown in England during the Renaissance.

That was another reason Winkie didn't like him. All he talked about was how they didn't have things back in the olden times. He went around the whole faire telling everyone what they were doing wrong. He did it to Clary and Ellie at least twice a week, which was just plain rude, especially because he was staying with the Hoglands for the summer.

But he wasn't at their stall today. He was at Mr. O'Reilly's taco shop next door. The two of them had been fighting since the start of the faire. The turnip man came back every day to "inspect" the place, and every day he and Mr. O got into a shouting match.

"Hear ye, hear ye, this stall has been declared

Historically Inaccurate!" Titus held up a small wooden sign with the letters *H* and *I* carved into it. "Tacos did not exist during the Renaissance. They were only introduced in the United States in 1905."

"Says who?" someone in the crowd asked. It sounded like Judy the corn on the cob lady.

Titus's forehead wrinkled. "What?"

"Who declared it? Was it Ted?" Phil, the Pickle on a Stick guy, stepped forward. "It's his faire, so he's the only one who can say anything about the stalls."

Mr. O grabbed the other end of the sign and pulled. "So this can go right in the trash can."

Titus stumbled forward, but he didn't let go of the sign. "But I counted thirty-nine infractions of the Privy Council guidelines yesterday. Including the recent addition of the corned beef and cabbage taco."

"There is no Privy Council," Ellie said. "That's just you making up rules that no one agreed to."

Titus wrenched his sign away from Mr. O and turned to Ellie. "You should be worried about your stall too."

"What's wrong with our stall?" Clary glared at him.

"Avocados."

"What about them?" Ellie said.

Titus turned to the crowd. "Do you know what they're putting in the goat's milk to make it ice cream?" He didn't wait for anyone to answer. "They're adding avocados to your concoctions, and the avocado wasn't introduced to the British Isles until the twentieth century."

It was quiet for a second, then the jester showed up with his lute. "What have we here?" He took one look at the avocados next to the ice-cream bucket,

then started singing "Guacamole ice cream" to the tune of "Greensleeves."

Mr. O'Reilly's face turned red. "You're just as bad, fool. No one gets a moment's peace with the two of you around." He reached out, pulled the jester into a headlock, and tried to yank his hat off. Winkie saw a big red birthmark high on the actor's head. It was shaped like a heart—just like the one between her nose holes.

"Hey, look!" Winkie called out to Horace, but he didn't pay any attention to her. He was totally focused on Ellie.

"Enough!" Clary slapped her hand down on a table, startling them all. "You"—she pointed at Mr. O—"let go of him or I'll report you to Ted. You"—she pointed at the jester—"get out of here or I'll break that lute into a million pieces." Then she turned to the turnip man. "And you, Wendell, stop being such a busybody."

He glared at her. "Please call me by my faire name, Titus."

She picked up an ice-cream scoop and pointed it at him. "Go back to your cart, Wendell! Right now! Or so help me, I'll have Lars and the kids pack your things and put them in the road."

Clary picked up her cell phone and started dialing.

"Fine." Wendell's eyes grew round, and he backed away. "I'll go, but I want you to know I'm going to report you for marketing fraud, and for having unclean animals in your food stall." He pointed at Winkie.

The world turned red.

"Did that skinny jerk just say I was dirty?" Winkie wrinkled her snout and got to her feet. "Nobody talks about me like that. I am the Cleaned-Up World Champion. I just won another round yesterday. That's it. This guy needs to learn some manners."

Wendell rushed away before she could leave the stall. As he hurried off, he passed the wandering minstrels, who were playing a raucous tune on their lutes.

"You can't play 'Thunderstruck' here! AC/DC is not on the approved list of music."

The minstrels just laughed and played louder.

"Oh, that boy!" Clary grumbled. "I should never have let Lars talk me into letting him stay with us this summer. He's just one bother after another. Took over my garden so he could grow turnips to sell here. Insists on sleeping in a hammock. And now look." She held up one of the ice-cream buckets. "He's used one of these for his gardening, so it's covered in dirt. I'll scrub it out, but I'm not sure we'll be able to use it again."

Ellie sighed. "That's one of the expensive Nantucket buckets too."

A tinkling of laughter outside the tent made Winkie's stomach twist. She picked up a pile of rocks and started chewing. This day just kept getting worse and worse.

3

Faire Play

Horace's plans to guard Eleanor were immediately challenged by the arrival of Blue Sparkles, the Hogland twins, and their older brother, Collin. Blue was a large sheep dog and one of several animals the twins had petnapped a couple weeks back. The last time Horace had seen him, he'd been covered in blue paint and silver glitter.

Horace nodded at him. "And how are you doing?"

"Excellent. I mean, I don't get steak everyday like I used to, but it's still good food." Blue paused and looked back at the Hoglands. "The only bad part is I'm sharing a room with a human named Wendell. He's the worst. He goes in and out all night, or he stays up writing in a little book he carries with him everywhere. I can't get any sleep."

"Sounds dreadful," Horace agreed.

Bunwinkle patted Blue on the back. "Poor thing. I can't imagine being stuck with that guy every day."

"Come on, Blue!" Linn and Nea called at the same time.

"Gotta go." The sheepdog hurried back to the twins, bumping into tables and benches as he went.

"You know, I think he looked better with the glitter," Bunwinkle said as they watched the group leave.

The rest of the day passed in relative peace. By evening Horace was in a better mood, and then

Dean arrived with a smile on his face and a small bag in his right hand.

"Why is he always bringing her things?" Horace grumbled. "She can get her own stuff. It's not as though she needs him to shower her with gifts."

But the gifts weren't for Eleanor, they were for Bunwinkle and him.

Dean opened the bag and pulled something out. "I made these especially for you two so you wouldn't eat the faire food or chew rocks."

"Oh my gosh, peanut butter popcorn balls!" Bunwinkle squealed.

So *this* was Dean's new game—he was trying to get to Eleanor through them. Well, Horace wasn't going to fall for it, no matter how delectable the popcorn balls looked. He sniffed in disapproval, catching a whiff of the treats.

They smelled even better than they looked.

He watched Bunwinkle take a bite.

"Uhhhhh." She smacked her lips. "This is the best thing I've ever eaten." She bumped his side. "Horace, you have to try one." She gobbled up another. "The peanut butter is so creamy and the popcorn is like . . . it's . . . it's perfect."

Horace's mouth watered. The popcorn did look perfect. He closed his eyes and turned away.

No, you don't want that villain's treats. Be strong.

Even though he couldn't see, he could smell, and his sniffer told him he had to have one. When he turned back there was a PB&P ball waiting for him.

Dean smiled and patted his head. "Here you go, boy."

That irritated Horace to the core of his being, but still he couldn't resist the treat. It smelled too good.

It was every bit as delightful as it smelled. Curse Dean and his culinary skills.

Eleanor squatted down next to them. "Thank you. It was nice of you to bring them goodies."

"You're welcome. I also came to offer my help at the stall."

"Actually, we're going to close up for the evening." Eleanor said as she stood up. "It was kind of a weird day and I think we could use a break."

"Well, let me help you clean up and then I'll

walk you home." Dean said it casually, but Horace knew this was the whole reason for the alpaca farmer's visit.

He should never have eaten those treats.

Dean and Eleanor moseyed their way back to the house, chatting the whole time. Horace made sure to walk in between them, but they barely seemed to notice. And Bunwinkle wasn't any help. She chatted with every animal on the faire grounds, leaving Eleanor's protection to him.

Everyone was getting too comfortable with Dean. Even the chicks were quiet when they walked by.

"Thanks for walking us home," Eleanor said when they reached the house. "Did you want to stay for dinner? Jennie's going to stay at her apartment in the city tonight to work on her costume, so it would just be us."

What was this? Eleanor was inviting him in?

Horace growled. "It's time for you to go."

Dean looked down at him, then up at Eleanor. "Maybe another time. I think I should let you all get some rest." He turned with a wave and walked in the other direction.

"Horace," Eleanor snapped. "Knock it off. I don't know what's gotten into you."

What had gotten into him? He was behaving like a perfect gentleman. It was that Dean person who was the problem. Horace had clearly shown the man that he was unwelcome, but he kept coming back. Another dog would have sensed Horace's dominance and left the area. Humans were so clueless.

Once Dean was out of sight, fatigue washed over Horace. It would be good to get into his bed and get comfortable. Unfortunately, Bunwinkle was situated between him and the pet door. Her

back half was in a kneeling position and her front half was stretched out in front of her. And she was making a humming noise

He frowned. "What are you doing?"

"Extended puppy." She hummed at him.

"What are you talking about? You're a piglet, not a puppy."

She raised her head and stared at him. "It's yoga. You were sitting right there when Shoo taught me how to do it. Remember? You kept telling me how great I was at it."

"You must be mistaken."

Bunwinkle shifted so that her front end was still down but her hind end was high in the air.

Horace continued, "I'm certain I would never have encouraged you to do something so undignified. Just look at yourself."

"Yoga is totally dignified. It comes from India and helps with the freak-outs. And it's way better than licking your legs."

Horace drew himself up to his full height. "I lick my legs to keep them clean. You know that. It's not because I have anxiety or nerves or whatever Dr. Schott says."

"Right."

"Never mind," Horace huffed. "I'll just do perimeter duty now."

He was halfway down the stairs when Bunwinkle called out, "Yoga would be good for your jealousy issues too."

The following morning arrived all too soon for Horace. Jennie came in the back door at 7:00 a.m.

Horace tried to open his eyes. He tried for a long time, but they simply wouldn't obey. He caught snippets of Eleanor and Jennie's conversation.

"Didn't have time to do the podcast . . . leave the yellow dress here . . . fix it later."

Suddenly something rough and wet that felt a lot like a pig's tongue licked his right eyelid.

"Wake up, Horace!" Bunwinkle shout-whispered in his face. "We're going to be late."

Horace groaned. "I don't want to go."

"Come on! It's Tournament Day!" Bunwinkle hopped on his bed and squealed. "They're going to have an archery contest and an ax-throwing competition and even a joust. It's going to be so exciting."

"None of that is real, you know," he grumbled. "It's not a real joust—they're just pretending. You'd understand that if you were more mature, like me."

Bunwinkle stuck her tongue out at him.

Clary was in a state when they arrived at the stall.

"The buckets are gone!" she said as soon as she saw them.

"What? All of them?" Eleanor rushed to Clary's side and lifted the tablecloth that hid the buckets.

Except it wasn't hiding anything today.

"No, just the ones we use for the goat milk ice cream—the Nantucket buckets."

Jennie squeezed Eleanor's arm. "I'll go get Ted."

"I don't understand," Eleanor said. "Who would take them?"

Horace leaned over and whispered, "Wendell."

"Whoa, get out of my head—I was just going to say that." Bunwinkle's eyes grew round.

Of course, Wendell wasn't the only villain at the faire. There was also that Uta creature.

He pressed on. "I suppose the bird also could have done it."

Bunwinkle shook her head. "I don't think it's her. She's too classy to steal other people's stuff."

Horace had to call upon all his good New England genes to control himself. Poor, deluded piglet, she actually thought birds had class. Sad.

"Yes . . . well, I can't speak to that. But I can say that Wendell was clearly upset yesterday after his failed attempt to shame Eleanor. And he had a use for the buckets—his gardening."

"Exactly," Bunwinkle agreed.

Out of nowhere, Dean ran in, a stack of buckets in his arms. "I found these in different places around the faire. It's not all of them, but I can run and find more while you wash these."

Eleanor looked confused. "How did you know

to look for them?"

"He was here when I came in," Clary said.

That was interesting. Horace hadn't really considered the human nuisance before. He could have taken the buckets, then returned with them like a hero so Eleanor would trust him. Oh, it was a brilliant plan.

"It wasn't Dean." Bunwinkle bumped Horace's side so hard he almost fell over.

"I didn't say it was," he snapped.

"But you're thinking it." She rolled her eyes. "You don't have a very good poke her face."

His forehead wrinkled in confusion. "What about my face?"

"It's easy to see what you're thinking. No one has to poke your face to get it to make an expression."

"I . . ." Horace stopped himself. Clearly she meant poker face, but it would certainly take more time than it was worth to correct her. "You know what? It doesn't matter. We'll use our pettective skills and find out who it was. Starting with Dean."

Bunwinkle stared at him. "Fine. We'll follow

him, but only until the tournament starts."

He groaned. Not this again.

"Don't you think a case is more important than some silly play?"

Her nostrils flared and she started tapping a hoof.

"All right," he sighed.

Fortunately, Dean was headed to the tournament as well. He asked Eleanor to join him, but at that moment a big family arrived at the stall and she had to stay.

Good thing too. Horace didn't want them spending any more time together.

"You know, we could have just walked down here with Dean," Bunwinkle said as they neared the tournament grounds.

"Tournament grounds" was a polite phrase for what was essentially a circle of dirt with bleachers on three sides and a shaded platform on the other.

"Where are we going to sit?" Horace asked. "It needs to be close enough to watch Dean, but far enough away that he doesn't notice us."

"Don't worry. Shoo's saving us a spot."

As if he'd heard them talking about him, Shoo's head peeked out from the bleacher directly across from the platform.

"Hey, guys, you got here just in time." He waved them over. "My lady and I didn't think you were gonna make it."

They ducked under the bleachers, where Shoo sat next to a white cat with an astonishing gray mustache.

Bunwinkle rushed over. "Princess, I didn't know you were gonna be here."

Princess Sofaneesba was another friend of

theirs. In fact, she and Shoo had helped them solve their last case.

"I couldn't miss Tournament Day," the cat said in her high-pitched voice.

"How did you get such good seats?" Bunwinkle asked. "I was sure we'd be staring at the backs of people's legs."

She was right. They did have an excellent view. Marred only by a pile of . . .

"Is that poop?" Bunwinkle asked.

Shoo grinned. "Yeah, but also no."

Horace put a paw to his forehead. He was definitely going to wind up with a headache.

"Shoobert." The princess stepped in. "They don't understand. Please explain what you mean."

"Anything for you, my lady. See, sometimes you gotta keep humans out of the way. And you know what humans hate?"

"Bodily waste?" Horace volunteered.

"Exactly. So all you gotta do is pile wet dirt on top of a dead fish to get something that looks and smells like poop. Then, voilà, automatic human repellent."

Princess Sofaneesba clapped her paws together.

"Isn't he clever?"

"He's . . . something," Horace said, turning his attention back to the arena. He had a clear view of the human nuisance—and also of Wendell, as it turned out. The young man sat one bench down and one section over from them, a notebook in one hand and a cell phone in the other. It looked like he was trying to take pictures of people without being seen.

After the fuss he'd raised about using items that weren't authentic, there he was using a cell phone. What a hypocrite!

"Hey, Shoo, what's in that bag?" Bunwinkle asked.

Horace glanced over at him and noticed a velvet bag at the raccoon's feet.

Shoo opened it up, a serious look on his face. "These are healing crystals They soothe all wounds. A tree spirit gave them to me."

"Tree spirit?" Horace couldn't help but ask.

Fortunately, just then the tournament began. Four men in tights and tunics stepped out and played a fanfare on trumpets almost as tall as they were. Horace noticed Uta Hawken on the shoulder of her human just outside the tournament ring. Well, this was his lucky day. All three suspects in one place.

"Rise for the presentation of Their Majesties, King Harold and Queen Beatrice."

The king with the fake beard walked in holding Jennie's hand. They smiled and waved.

"Whoa, that dress is sweet. Way better than the one she wore last time." Shoo said.

"Jennie made it herself," Horace informed him.

Princess Sofaneesba nodded. "The king's costume is new as well. His pants are much redder and they have a new pattern on them. Diamonds, I think. Oh, but his shoes don't match."

"I didn't even notice the pattern on his pants." Bunwinkle nudged his side. "Did you?"

"Yes, indeed," he said. Truthfully, he couldn't say much about the costumes from the previous tournament because he'd blocked it from his mind.

It had been a terrible disappointment. The script was terrible. You could barely hear the actors speak. And one man actually fell off his horse in the middle of a speech. Frankly, it had been embarrassing to watch.

"Greeting, loyal subjects," Queen Beatrice called out. "We are honored to be with you today."

Everyone clapped and Bunwinkle stomped her hooves.

The king spoke next. "Today we shall have a tournament in honor of my beloved wife. A display of talent worthy of her beauty."

Jennie curtsied to him then turned back to the audience. "And I shall offer a prize to the winner of the joust." She held up a white piece of fabric. "My pearl-studded handkerchief."

The king looked startled. "Now, my dear, let us not be hasty. That was my gift to you. It is far too fine a prize. Why don't you offer a lock of your hair instead?"

"But—" Jennie looked confused for a moment but then she smiled and nodded at the king.

"Now let us have a song to begin the festivities."

A song meant only one thing—the jester.

Horace's head immediately started to ache.

Sure enough, the fool danced onto the stage strumming the lute. His playing was accompanied by the bells sewn onto his costume.

"Come, ye lords and ladies, come along with me," the jester sang to the tune of "Greensleeves."

"This is a sweet tune," Shoo said, bobbing his head in time with the song.

A tune that went on far too long. Horace would have stuffed cotton in his ears if he'd had any. Finally, after what felt like an eternity, the bells stopped ringing and the jester shouted, "Now please welcome Millicent the juggler."

Horace groaned. Not a juggler.

Well, at least he had something to distract him. He would focus on the suspects. Watch for any suspicious behavior. All he needed to do was keep his eyes open.

4

Horse Feathers

The tournament was the most exciting thing that had ever happened to Winkie. Well, except for the time she attacked Mal. And the time she got pignapped. And the time she was held hostage.

It's just that it was so *fancy*. Everyone wore beautiful clothes, even the boys. Winkie would have loved to wear Jennie's blue dress. She would never

admit it to Horace, but she really wanted to be a princess.

Speaking of her brother, he was sound asleep on the ground next to her. How was that even possible? The tournament had been loud, especially during the jousting competition, but he'd just kept on snoring.

She pressed the ticklish spot on his side.

His eyes fluttered open. "Hmm."

"It's over."

He yawned and nodded as his eyes closed again.

"No, don't go back to sleep, we have to investigate. Remember?" She shook him. Then she shook him harder. "Hey! Wake up!"

But nothing worked. He slept through it all, just like Smith had the other day.

"Doesn't he look sweet like that?" Princess Sofaneesba said.

Shoo looked around her. "Aw, leave him. Little dude needs his rest. It'll help with his inner harmonies."

Winkie sighed. "But he wanted to do some investigating. Someone sabotaged our ice-cream stall."

They all watched Horace sleep for a second and then Shoo said, "We can help you."

To be safe, they decided to follow all three suspects. Princess Sofaneesba took Dean. Apparently, there was a cat named Mittens who hung out near his house and might be able to help. Shoo took Wendell. The raccoon felt they had the right vibatiousness, whatever that was, with one another. Also, as he pointed out, Wendell might notice Winkie since he'd seen her before.

That left Winkie with Uta Hawken.

At first there wasn't much for her to do. After the show, the hawk and her human, Ted, stayed on the tournament grounds chatting with people. Finally, everyone cleared out, and Uta and Ted headed back behind the stage.

Winkie tried one more time to wake her brother, but it was no use.

"I'll be back soon," she whispered before hurrying after her suspect.

The backstage area looked a lot like a campground. There were tents everywhere. There was also a big sign that said STAFF ONLY, which

Winkie ignored. You couldn't be a good pet-tective if you stayed out of every place they told you to. Plus she was dying to see all the cool stuff backstage, like the dresses and crowns.

When she caught up to Uta and her human, they were standing by a white pickup truck talking to the jester. The two men were glaring at each other, but Uta kept turning her head as though she was looking for something.

"You can't park this here," Ted said.

"What difference does it make where I park the truck? I'm not in anyone's way."

"You're in the way of my legal business." Ted grabbed something from the back of the truck and held it up. "And why do you have this?"

The jester raised his hands and said, "Hey, talk to Louie. I didn't have anything to do with that."

Louie? Which one of them was that? Winkie hadn't heard of anyone called Louie. And what was Ted holding up? She squinted to see better, then gasped. It was one of the Nantucket buckets.

All three of them—Ted, Uta, and the

jester—turned to look in her direction. Shoot, she hadn't meant to be so loud.

"Uta, perimeter duty," Ted ordered, his eyes darting around.

The hawk nodded and flew up into the air. Winkie quickly ducked under the edge of the closest tent, which turned out to be Jennie's dressing room. Jennie was in the middle of a conversation with the king.

"My dear, you simply cannot make a change to the script at the last minute. Especially if it involves giving away a prop."

Jennie shook her head. "I wasn't giving it away. It's not like I offered this thing to an audience member."

"It's like the dress. You said you were going to fix it and bring it back, but you haven't done that."

She put the handkerchief in the king's hand. "Take it. And I'll bring the dress back tomorrow. Okay? Can we go out and do our jobs now?"

Their voices faded as if they were walking away. Winkie wanted to go after them. But first she needed to get out from under the tent. The only problem was she couldn't find the way out. Geez, how much material did they use to make these things?

She finally found an escape route just as a couple of people stopped near the tent. Ugh! She was never going to get back before Horace woke up.

"No, we haven't found them yet."

That voice sounded familiar, but Winkie couldn't be sure who it belonged to. The tent material was making it difficult to hear clearly. She finally found the edge of the tent and scrambled out from under it—almost getting stepped on by Wendell the turnip guy. Luckily he didn't notice her. He was too busy taking pictures with his cell phone.

What was he doing there? And why was he using modern technology? Something about that guy didn't add up.

When she got back, Shoo and the princess were waiting beside Horace, who was somehow still asleep.

"I thought you were going to follow Wendell," Winkie said. "He almost stepped on me."

"I did," Shoo said. "I followed the guy back to his vegetable cart. I watched him for five minutes and all he did was write in a little notebook."

"Is that all?" Winkie asked.

"Pretty much. The dude puts off a negative energy that repels people. No one even slowed down to look at his turnips." Shoo wiped his nose on the back of his arm. "I kinda felt sorry for him."

Winkie turned to the white cat. "What about you, Princess?"

"I followed Dean back to his farm. He didn't do anything unusual, so I tracked down my friend Mittens. She lives at Barton Orchards, but she's a bit of a roamer. It's the insomnia, you see. It hits her and all she can do is walk until she's tired enough to sleep."

"I get it. It stinks when you can't sleep." Winkie had that insomnia thing sometimes too.

"She said Dean was home last night. Apparently, he's home pretty much every night."

Winkie nodded. Dean had never really been a suspect in her mind. Uta hadn't either, but they had to check them out to be sure. But what was going on with Wendell?

"You investigated without me?"

Horace's furious voice surprised them all, but Winkie was the only one who jumped.

For the rest of the day Horace barely talked to her. And he wouldn't listen to her even a little bit. She tried to explain what they'd found out a bunch of times. But every time she opened her mouth, he put his paws over his ears or walked away.

He kept it up all night. Even after they got home.

"How many times do I have to say I'm sorry, Horace?" she asked after hours of the silent treatment.

No answer. Big surprise.

She got why he was mad—she wouldn't want to be left out either. But it wasn't *her* fault he wouldn't wake up when it was time to investigate. Besides, they had found solid evidence that eliminated two of their suspects. Which Horace would know if he'd listen. But he was always too busy talking to her like she was a baby and telling her to grow up. Geez. Sometimes it was hard to be a sister.

And, honestly, it made her heart hurt.

At 10:00 p.m. he got up and stretched.

"Are you going somewhere?" she asked.

"Perimeter duty."

She hopped up. "I'll come."

Horace didn't so much as look at her. "No. I want to go alone."

He came back a little while later. As he climbed into bed, Winkie whispered, "You know, Horace, you're a great brother, but when you get super angry you stop talking to me and it feels awful. It would be better if you yelled, because at least I would know you still loved me."

The next morning Winkie woke up to the sound of the garbage disposal. Why would Ellie run it so early?

"Ah-hem."

There it was again.

Winkie opened her eyes only to see Horace standing in front of her bed. "Ah-hem."

So it wasn't the garbage disposal.

Horace took a deep breath then said, "I thought a lot about what you said last night, and I believe I owe you an apology."

Her ears perked up. What was this?

"John Adams said, 'No man is entirely free from weakness and imperfection in this life.' And I am no exception. It's difficult for me to express my emotions, so I keep them to myself. But you've shown me that there are downsides to that." He paused and cleared his throat again. "I hope you can forgive me."

It was always like this. He kept his feelings all bottled up and then they exploded. If only he would talk to her.

"Yeah," she sighed. "I forgive you."

"And, uh, I want you to know I always love you."
His voice was gruff and his face was scrunched up
as if he was trying not to cry.

And just like that the pain her heart disappeared.

She kissed him on the side of the face. "I love
you too."

"All right, now that we've cleared that up, I say
we go eat breakfast."

"Hold on. Before we eat, I need to do my yoga."

Horace groaned.

Winkie centered her thoughts and went
through her poses. She was just finishing when
Jennie crossed through the room. "Yoga, huh?
You should try piggy Pilates." She winked at
them, then yelled, "Hey, I've got to meet some-
body at the faire. I'm going on ahead. I'll see you
later."

After breakfast, they were off to the faire again.
As they walked over, Winkie told Horace everything that had happened the day before, including
the parts about the bucket and Wendell.

At the end of her report, he nodded and said,

"Well, I hadn't really suspected the bird, but I'm not quite ready to eliminate Dean."

"Did you miss the part where I said the jester had our bucket and Titus 'I wish I lived in ye olden times' Asparagus was taking pictures?" she asked in a snotty voice.

Horace tilted his head up and sniffed. "I heard you. I'm simply saying that Dean is still a viable suspect."

Winkie turned her head so he wouldn't see her roll her eyes—and ran into the back of Ellie's leg.

"Ouch." She rubbed her snout on her leg. "What happen—" Winkie ran out of words when she saw what had made Ellie stop suddenly. Their stall was completely destroyed. The tables had been knocked over and broken apart. Buckets were filled with mud and garbage. The chest freezer was on its side, milk and fruit crushed into the ground in front of it. And as if that wasn't enough, someone had spray-painted the words TIME TO PAY! all over the canvas walls.

It felt like someone had grabbed Winkie and squeezed all the air out of her.

As the three of them stood there taking in the

damage, Clary showed up with the twins, Linn and Nea.

"What on earth?" Clary gasped.

Ellie looked over at her. "They destroyed everything."

Clary ran a hand through her hair. "I don't understand. Why would anyone do this? We're not some Fortune 500 company. And what does

'Time to Pay' even mean?"

"Look, they got another stall over there too." Nea Hogland pointed to the scone shop across the way.

"And I see another wrecked one up by the Pickle on a Stick stand," Linn said.

"How many stalls did the villains destroy?" Horace muttered under his breath.

A lot, by the looks of things.

"You don't think Wendell would do something like this?" Ellie asked.

"What would he gain from it?" But Clary didn't sound exactly sure of that.

"What happened?" Dean stood outside the tent holding a tray with two cups of coffee.

He looked as stunned as Winkie felt.

"Someone is playing a prank," Ellie said. "It's nothing."

"This is not nothing," Horace and Dean said at the same time. They had the same determined expression on their faces. They were so much alike. If only Horace could see that.

"Ellie! Ellie!" Jennie raced into the tent and skidded to a halt in front of her friend. "Oh my gosh, they got you too."

"Oh no," Ellie said. "They didn't touch the backstage area, did they?"

Jennie's shoulders drooped. "Whoever did this destroyed things everywhere, including my dressing room where I had all my clothing and costumes."

"Something weird is going on here, and we need to find out what." Winkie whispered to her brother.

"Absolutely." He held up his paw. "Pet-tectives investigate?"

Winkie bumped his paw with her hoof. "Pet-tectives investigate."

While the humans cleaned up the mess, Winkie and Horace slipped out of the stall.

"We'll start with the turnip man," Horace said.

Winkie had never seen him so serious before. Whoever had done this had better watch out.

Wendell—also known as Titus Asparagus, also known as the Merchant of Vegetables—was easy to find. His cart was the only quiet spot in the whole faire. Even he wasn't there.

"He's probably bothering another vendor," Winkie said.

Horace nodded. "Let's look around before he comes back."

There wasn't much around the cart. Just a couple baskets of turnips, a money box that was locked, and a notebook. Winkie opened it and started to read.

Pickle on a Stick* Infractions
Drinking from a plastic bottle in front of customers
Used cell phone 28 times
Turkey pickle is an abomination
Note: Speak to Ted about banning them from the park
*First time with the faire. Knows nothing of the history of the group.

She turned a couple pages, but they were all pretty much the same. The only stall this guy liked was his own. Pretty hypocritical of the guy to get upset about people using cell phones when he was doing it too.

"What have you found?" Horace's face touched hers.

"Not much."

"Me neither." Horace glanced around. "Maybe someone saw something. Look, Mal and Minnie are right over there. They have a perfect view of Wendell's comings and goings."

Winkie frowned. Why did it have to be Mal? Something weird always happened when they were around him. And what was he even doing at the faire?

"Fine. I'll go, but if it even looks like he's about to headbutt me I'm outta there."

Mal saw them coming and grinned. "Och, 'bout time ye come to see us. We've got news."

"Mah, sooooomethinggggg isn't riiiiight here," Minnie added.

"I knew it!" Horace's ear went to full alert. "What did you see?"

"First, I seen a man wearing a kilt."

"What was he doing?" Horace asked.

"Doin'? Doin'?" Mal's eyes got all fiery. "He was wearing socks, sandals, and a Hawaiian shirt! A sure villain if I've ever seen one."

67

And there was the weirdness. Who cared what a person wore with a kilt?

Minnie sighed. "Iiiit was a siiiiight."

"A blasphemy. Ye'd never catch me wearing something like that."

"You're a goat. You can't wear sandals," Winkie pointed out.

"'Tis nae the point. Neither goat nor man should dishonor the kilt. Ye ken?"

Winkie sighed. "No, I'm Winkie. I don't know why you keep calling me Ken."

Minnie threw her head back and laughed. "Keeeeeeeen! Gooood one."

Horace held up a paw and cleared his throat. "Ah-hem. Bunwinkle and I are here on serious business. There has been sabotage at the ice-cream stall and we're searching for the culprit. We believe Wendell may be involved."

"Yer saying the daft lad selling the tumshie was up to mischief?"

That was the thing about talking with Mal. All the words sounded familiar but nothing he said made sense. Winkie looked over at Horace. His head was tilted to the side and his eyes were squinted as though he was concentrating really hard.

"Yes?" Horace didn't sound sure about his answer, though.

Mal nodded his head. "Could be. 'Tis hard to say. The lad is hardly ever here, and he talks to no one. Not the blethering type, that one. Only person I seen him talk to is that eejit with the bells."

Horace nodded, which hopefully meant he

69

understood what Mal had said. Winkie was still trying to figure out what a tumshie was.

"Thank you for your help."

"Nae a problem."

As soon as they were out of earshot, Winkie stopped her brother. "Why did you thank him? Did he tell us something important?"

"If I understood correctly, he said that Wendell is never around, which is exactly what Blue Sparkles said." Horace wove his way through the humans walking along the path moving closer to the Merchant of Vegetables cart. Winkie followed close behind him.

Winkie sighed. "That doesn't prove he did it though, does it?"

"Unfortunately, it doesn't."

Horace found a shady spot and dropped to the ground. He looked around, then started licking his legs.

"If only we could talk to someone who can move around freely and stays here through the night," he said between licks.

"You called?"

5

An Insult to Good Manners

That dreadful bird was back. Horace called upon all his proper New England manners to speak with her.

"Greetings . . . bird."

Yes. That was good and civil.

The creature had the temerity to look down her beak at him. "Cur."

"Why you filthy, feathered—"

Bunwinkle stepped on his paw and shook her head. But she was all smiles and sweetness when she spoke to the horrid creature.

"Uta! Great performance in the play this week. You were awesome."

"Of course. I'm a professional."

Horace opened his mouth to reply, but Bunwinkle cut him off again.

"And you're looking fantastic. Did you do something different to your feathers?"

The hawk preened. "Why, yes. I've been eating more rodents, and the nutrients have made my feathers shinier. Thank you for noticing."

"Oh." Bunwinkle's face turned green and her smile fell. Hah! Served her right. What did she expect from a bird? She was out of her depth. Horace would have to step in.

"All right, Hawken, no more of your disgusting stories. Tell us what you know about the attacks on the faire last night." You had to be firm with feathered creatures or they would flit from topic to topic.

"Would you stop being rude?" Bunwinkle whispered out of the side of her mouth. "We could use her help."

"*I'm* being rude? She called me a cur. That's the height of rudeness."

The foul fowl must have overheard them because her next words had a different tone. "It's true. And while you are of such low consequence that you couldn't possibly know what is proper, I *do* know. However, I have no idea what you're talking about. What attacks?"

Didn't know what proper was? How dare she?

He opened his mouth, but Bunwinkle hit him with her shoulder hard enough to leave a bruise.

Deep breath. Rise above, Horace.

"Look around," he managed to say through gritted teeth. "See all the people picking their goods off the ground, or what's left of them?"

Uta whipped her head around, her eyes growing wider and wider. "This can't be. I've been flying patrols day and night so that nothing like this would happen."

"Hey, that's just like us doing patrol duty, right, Horace?" Bunwinkle said.

Horace ignored the comment. Surely he had nothing in common with that wretched creature.

"So how did you miss someone doing all this?" Horace asked. He couldn't keep the disdain from his voice. Hawken praised herself constantly, and it was pleasing to see her brought back down to earth.

"I . . . I was following that horrible busybody, the Merchant of Vegetables, if you must know."

Bunwinkle smiled. "That's who we came to ask you about. So did he do it?"

The bird gave Bunwinkle a pitying look. "I wouldn't have been surprised by the damage if he had."

"Oh, right. So what was he doing, then?"

"Nothing. He went to that hovel where he's renting a room and stayed there all night. Ted watched about ten minutes of the video, then turned it off."

"Wait, did your human tell you to watch Wendell?" Bunwinkle asked.

Uta shifted and looked uncomfortable. "Well, no. But that young man has been highly critical, especially for someone who's never been involved in a Renaissance Faire before. And he wanders quite a bit—all through the faire and the surrounding fields. Ted told me to keep an eye out for trouble and the Merchant of Vegetables looks like trouble to me."

"I don't trust this bird for a moment," Horace whispered to Bunwinkle, "but there may be a way to get some good information from her." To Uta he said, "You said something about a video."

"Yes. Ted can't come with me, of course, so he's attached a small camera to my leg."

Bunwinkle tapped her front hooves excitedly. "Can we see the recordings from last night?"

The hawk studied them for a moment then sighed. "Oh, all right. But I only have a few minutes. Ted will surely need me to help him with this."

Uta flew up and Horace found himself chasing after her. How embarrassing. She led them outside the faire, to a little camper.

"Before we enter I must insist you be on your best behavior."

Only the prospect of seeing who had ransacked their stall stopped Horace from replying. Instead he forced himself to smile. "Of course."

She opened the door for them, and they climbed in. The interior of the camper was decorated with posters of Uta in different plays. It was like a shrine to the bird. Horace shuddered.

"Over here." She perched on the table next to a laptop. She tapped a few keys, and a video started to play on the screen.

"Why is it all green?" Bunwinkle asked.

"It's in night-vision mode. Otherwise Ted wouldn't be able to see anything."

It wasn't easy to watch. The images were

unsteady and passed by very fast, which made sense since the camera was attached to a bird. That didn't make it any less frustrating, though.

"I can't tell what anything is, can you?" Bunwinkle whispered.

"No."

The hawk could. She pointed out several places to them, but there wasn't anything suspicious.

"I am sorry. But it seems I wasn't at the stall when the damage occurred."

Horace wasn't surprised. He hadn't truly believed she could help them.

"Hey, what's that?" Bunwinkle hit the keyboard with her snout and the image froze.

In the grainy, green light four human legs were visible.

"That's from a few nights ago." Uta tilted her head with a frown. Suddenly her eyes grew big and she gasped. "Caliban."

"Isn't that the stuff Ellie uses for bug bites and other itchies?"

Horace shook his head. "No, that's calamine. It's lotion."

Uta tsked her tongue. "Caliban is a monster

with four legs and one eye, from *The Tempest*. But it can't be. He isn't real." She put a wing up to her beak, like she was going to cry or sneeze. "I performed *The Tempest*, you know—at the Globe Theatre with Dame Judy as Prospero. I received rave reviews, and she said I was the best hawk she'd had the privilege to work with."

Horace's right eye started to twitch. He put a paw up to stop it. "Look, we don't have time to hear your reviews."

But the bird wasn't listening. She was deep in thought.

He turned his attention back to the video. There was something familiar about one of the sets of legs. Was it the pants? They were puffy and there was a pattern of some sort on them. All of a sudden it hit him. He knew those pants, and so did Bunwinkle.

"Recognize anything?" he asked her.

She leaned close, her snout almost touching the computer screen. "Those are Wendell's pants."

"But according to the bird, he was home last night. He couldn't have messed everything up here."

Bunwinkle scratched her head. "There are four legs there, so Wendell must have a partner. Maybe they did it while he hung out at the Hoglands'."

"But why?" Horace asked.

"To trick Ted into thinking he wasn't involved?"

She didn't sound very convinced, and Horace couldn't blame her. The whole thing was just too confusing.

Bunwinkle leaned close to the screen again. "There's something else down in the corner there. I think it's a pair of hooves."

"The horses!" they said in unison.

Uta turned off the video. "I think it's time you were on your way."

For once Horace agreed with the bird.

The horses were in a set of stalls next to the tournament ring. Jones was asleep when they got there, but Smith was wide awake. Awake and agitated.

"Thought you two would never come to visit," the black-spotted horse said.

Bunwinkle nodded. "It's good to see you too."

"Something is wrong with my brother!"

"That's a bit harsh," Horace said. Of course,

he didn't entirely disagree. Jones *was* an oddball who believed in sprites and aliens, but he had a good heart.

"I think he got bit by something," Smith went on. "He's got a sickly look and he does nothing but sleep."

The gray horse looked fine to Horace. He was a bit thinner and his hooves were coated in dried mud, but so were Smith's.

"You've been sleeping a lot too," Horace pointed out. "Especially during the day."

Smith's muzzle wrinkled up like he smelled skunk. "Nonsense. I never nap. I might rest my eyes for a few minutes, but I tell ya I'm wide awake. Unlike my brother here."

"I know what it is!" Bunwinkle shouted. "He's got orange disease."

"You mean Lyme disease." Horace corrected her.

"That's the one." She leaned closer, her eyes round. "You get it from ticks. I watched this whole show about it. This famous actress got it and almost . . ." She looked up at Smith, then whispered to Horace. "She almost died."

They all stared at Jones, who chose that moment to sneeze all over them.

Smith teared up. "Poor Jones."

Horace wiped his face on Bunwinkle's side. "Oh, for pity's sake, he doesn't have Lyme disease and there's nothing wrong with him that getting back to the Homestead wouldn't cure."

Jones opened his eyes and looked around at everyone. "You guys having a party without me?"

He chuckled at his own joke, though no one else did.

"Brother, we're worried about you," Smith said.

"Yeah," Bunwinkle agreed. "You got ticks and now you're gonna die."

To Horace's surprise Jones laughed. "Shoot, I'm fit as a fiddle. Just a little tired on account of working all night. You've been sleeping more too, you know."

Smith snorted. "What are you talking about? All we do is pull carts of kids around the faire."

"You really don't remember?" Jones asked.

"Remember what?" his brother demanded.

Jones lifted his head, looked around, then lowered his muzzle. "We're not supposed to talk about this. We're sworn to secrecy."

Here it came—another nonsensical conspiracy theory. What would it be this time? Fire breathing bumblebees? Godzilla?

"We're working for Santa Claus."

Huh. That was a new one.

"No way," Bunwinkle said. "Santa doesn't work in the summer."

The old gray horse gave her a pitying look. "Of

course he does. You don't think he can do all that work in a single month, do you? He's got to work all year long."

"Bunwinkle," Smith cut in. "Don't listen to this old fool. We're not working for anyone but that fella who runs the faire."

"Right," Jones said. "Because that fella is working with Santa too."

Smith squeezed his lips together and rolled his eyes.

"What about the elves?" Bunwinkle asked. She was clearly having a hard time letting go of this nonsense.

"What about 'em?"

Her mouth fell open. "Where are they? Why aren't they here helping?"

"Reckon they're busy making toys and such up at the North Pole," Jones said as though this was a perfectly rational conversation.

"Aha!" Bunwinkle's eyes gleamed. "So you admit that there is a North Pole?"

Horace looked up at Smith, who just shook his head.

"Never said there wasn't."

"Fine. Then tell me this. Why would Santa Claus use horses for his work when he's got reindeer?"

"Aw, heck, you don't think one of them fancy creatures would come down here and pull a cart around, do you? They're used to flying everywhere."

"And he's not using reindeer because he isn't here," Smith said.

Bunwinkle ignored his comment and continued to stare at Jones, tapping a hoof on the ground. "I want to meet him."

Horace rolled his eyes. "Oh, for heaven's sake, Smith is right. They're not working for Santa. Something much more nefarious is going on."

Jones stomped his hoof. "You see here, young feller. I would know if I was a part of something underhanded. I am not. I'm working for the man playing jingle bells in his red suit."

"What's he got you doing?" Bunwinkle asked. "Digging up coal for bad kids and headbutting goats? Carrying gifts?"

Jones shook his head. "Hauling carrots."

Horace shouldn't have been surprised, but

he was. Usually Jones's stories were consistent. If it was pirates, they were doing pirate-related things. Same with angels and ghosts. But there was simply no way to connect Santa with carrots.

And he clearly wasn't the only one having a hard time with this little twist. Bunwinkle's expression had changed from delighted to doubtful.

"I don't get it," she said. "Why would Santa need carrots?"

Smith's expression turned thoughtful. "Carrots?"

"Are you remembering, brother?"

"And we were looking for them in the field just outside the faire grounds," Smith said slowly.

"That's it." Jones grinned. "And do you remember who took us out there?"

Everyone waited quietly while Smith tried to remember. "Can't say as I do. But I know it wasn't no Santa Claus."

"Ugh, you're impossible," Jones huffed.

Horace took this as their cue to leave. "Well, gentlemen, it's time for Bunwinkle and me to head back to the ice-cream stand. You have a good day."

6

The Lady Doth Protest
Too Much

"Hey," Winkie said, as Horace pushed her away from the horse stalls. "I still have a bunch of questions to ask about Santa!"

"No, you don't."

She opened her mouth to say something just as he pushed her again, and she wound up biting her tongue.

"Ow." She frowned at him. "You're gonna get coal in your stocking when Santa finds out." She stuck out her tongue and tried to check it.

"For the last time," Horace sniffed, "they didn't see Santa. That was just another one of

Jones's stories."

Poor Horace. He really was the grumpiest dog in the whole world. Imagine hearing the name Santa Claus and not getting excited.

"I think we should check it out just to make sure," Winkie said as Horace moved to block her way back to the horses.

"No. We have to get back to the stall before anyone notices we're gone. Santa may not be here, but Ellie is, and I know she'll be upset if we get into trouble again. Besides, they may have learned something about the culprits."

She hated to admit it, but he had a good point. "Okay, you can stop now. I'll go back to the tent."

"Excellent," Horace said. He came up beside her and they started walking again.

They were quiet on account of having to dodge feet and legs on the path. They snuck into the stall about half a second before Ellie said, "Has anyone seen Horace and Bunwinkle?"

Dean glanced over at them, then back at Ellie. "They're right there."

Winkie did her best to look innocent, yawning and stretching as if she'd just woken up. Horace, on the other hand, looked like he'd committed every crime ever. His eyes darted all over the place and he breathed in and out really fast. He was going to give them away.

"Stop that." Winkie shook her head. "Act normal."

"This is normal."

She sighed. "You need to be chill like me. My tongue is killing me, but I'm still chill."

Horace rolled eyes. "Your tongue is fine. You just need to focus on something else." He flopped down beside her and started licking his legs. *"Like me."*

Her tongue really did hurt, though. Something yellow and shiny in the dirt caught her eye. It was one of Shoo's healing crystals. Oh, and there was another one! That's what she needed. They would definitely help her feel better. All she had to do was suck on them.

* * *

Uta's human and the owner of the faire showed up a few minutes later. Ted quietly walked around the stall, taking in all the damage.

"Was anyone hurt?" His voice was so quiet Winkie could barely hear him.

Ellie shook her head. "No, we're all fine. But they destroyed all our stock and equipment. That was a lot of money we lost."

He nodded, his face super serious. "I'm so sorry, Eleanor. I'll reimburse you for everything."

"Jennie too?" Ellie asked.

"What did they do to Jennie?" Ted's face turned white.

Clary sighed. "They shredded all her costumes, even the ones she brought from home."

"But she's okay, right? No one hurt her?"

Dean answered him. "She's fine. She went back to her apartment to get another dress. She's determined to do her job."

Ted ran a hand through his hair and sighed. "Might be better if she didn't." He shook Eleanor's hand, then Clary's. "Let me know how much you lost and I'll get you the money. And stay safe. I'll look into this, I promise."

After he walked away, Clary gave a sad laugh. "He's never going to figure out what happened."

Ellie walked over and wrapped an arm around her friend. "I'm sorry about all this, Clary. I really thought the stall would be a good way to have fun and make some money."

"I know. Me too. I thought it would be just like when we did lemonade stands during your summer visits."

"You know what? We need to have some fun. Let's go see the faire. We'll get the stall up and running again tomorrow."

"We'd like that, wouldn't we, girls?"

"Yes, Mama," the twins answered at the same time.

"Can I come along?" Dean asked.

Ellie smiled at him. "Of course."

Horace stood up tall, head up, ears up. "We're going on full alert for this. Focus only on keeping anyone from getting too close to Eleanor."

Winkie nodded, but she wasn't really listening to her brother. All she could think about was the twins. She knew they weren't going to pignap her again, but she never really felt safe when they were around.

Please let these healing crystals work on anxiety.

In the end Winkie had tons of fun, even with the twins there. Horace didn't, though. He low-key growled at everyone who got within in five feet of Ellie and full-on barked whenever Dean opened his mouth.

The whole group wound up at the tournament field ten minutes before the court play was about to begin.

"Can we stay, Mama?" Linn Hogland asked.

Nea hopped up and down and pleaded, "Please. We'll be good."

"What do you think, Eleanor?" Clary asked.

"Sure. After today we'll probably be too busy with the booth to see it anyway."

They looked around and found seats right up front.

"I wonder why these haven't been taken," Clary said.

"Ewww, poop." The twins jumped back, almost stepping on Winkie.

She squealed and ran to Horace's side. Good thing she had her healing crystals, otherwise she would have been kinda freaked out. Yoga would've been better, but there was no room to do it here.

"No problem, girls," Dean said, picking up an empty drink cup and scraping the fake poop back behind the bleachers. "There you go. Nothing to worry about now."

From underneath they heard Shoo's voice. "Aw, man, now I'm gonna smell like fish."

Before Winkie could check on him, the jester danced onto the stage.

"Wow, he looks terrible," she whispered to Horace. "Do you think he ever washes that costume?"

"Not from the look of it." Horace wrinkled his nose.

The jester turned to the audience and held a finger up to his lips, then tiptoed to the king's throne. He reached behind it and pulled out a lute.

"Perhaps a song while we wait for their most royal travesties, I mean, majesties." He sat down on the throne and started playing "Greensleeves."

"Alas, my friends, my lord's a twit.
He knows not fashion, not one little bit.
His taste in color is my pet peeve,
for his purple shirt has two green sleeves.
Green sleeves on a purple shirt.
I want to drag it right through the dirt."

Everyone laughed and clapped as he sang.

"At least his songs have gotten better," Winkie said to Horace.

Suddenly two men wearing different colored cloaks ran onto the stage. Each one held a small birdcage. They didn't seem to see the jester, but he saw them and stopped playing.

From offstage Jennie shouted, "Villains! How dare you steal my canaries?"

Horace snorted. "That's ridiculous. No one would ever steal birds."

"You said she wouldn't be home!" the first thief, who wore a red cape, said.

The second thief, in a green cape, ran to one side of the stage and acted like he was looking out a window. "She was supposed to be away at a ball."

"I knew it was a mistake to come alone," thief

one said. "I told you we needed a lookout."

"This isn't the regular show," Horace whispered.

"Maybe they do a new one each week?" Winkie offered.

Horace shook his head. "I don't think so. Look at the other faire people."

He was right. The rest of the troupe stood to one side of the stage watching the show. Some of them were holding binders and talking loudly. Everyone looked confused.

Uta Hawken and Ted were a part of the group. It's hard to tell what birds are thinking because their beaks always make them look angry, but it seemed to Winkie that the hawk was worried. So was Ted. He kept running his hand through his hair while he watched.

Thief two opened his pretend window and peeked his head through it. "We couldn't wait for our lookout. We owe Oats and Mayes too much money. Come on now. We'll drop down and sneak around to the horses."

Oats and Mayes. Why did that sound familiar?

Jennie rushed onto the stage in a pretty blue

dress, holding a huge crossbow. "You won't be going anywhere."

There was a loud clang of lute strings and bells. The jester and his lute had fallen off the throne onto the stage. His eyes were real big, and he kept opening and closing his mouth like a fish out of water.

Wait, was that part of the show?

The performers kept going like nothing had happened. Jennie took aim and shot the crossbow. The audience gasped as the arrow flew across the stage, but then it bounced off the rear end of the thief in the red cloak and everyone laughed.

"The arrow is made of rubber. How clever." Princess Sofaneesba's voice floated up to them.

"How did you like that, you knaves?" Jennie shot another arrow, barely missing the king as he rushed onto the stage. His hat was on crooked and his red suit wasn't zipped up all the way so you could see his undershirt. And he'd forgotten his fake beard.

"What is the meaning of this?" he asked, puffing for breath.

Jennie loaded another arrow. "They're trying

to steal my precious canaries. The ones you gave me when we married."

The king frowned like she was talking another language. "Canaries?"

"Yes." She nodded with a grin. "And now they're going to pay for it."

She shot the arrow and the king stumbled back, tripping over the jester and landing with a loud thump on his throne.

Jennie turned to see if he was okay, and the thieves used it as a chance to escape through the pretend window.

The audience laughed again.

"What is going on?" Winkie whispered to Horace. "This got weird."

"Maybe it's avant-garde theater. A nonlinear, experimental thing." Shoo offered from under the bleachers. "Or something surreal like *Waiting for Godot*."

Dang it. The show was great before. Why did they have to mess with it?

"Blast! They've escaped!" Jennie lowered the crossbow and stomped her foot. "If only—"

But nobody got to hear what she was going to

say because a bug chose that moment to fly into one of Winkie's nose holes. She gasped, accidentally inhaling the crystals she'd been sucking on, and started choking. Loudly.

She tried to breathe but no air got in. "Hunh-hunh."

Horace gave her a worried look. "What happened? What's wrong?"

Winkie tried to cough, but you need air to cough and she didn't have any. Her heart beat faster and her legs started to shake. And she got even louder.

People all around them turned to stare. Even the actors were focused on her. She would have been embarrassed if she hadn't been so worried about passing out.

Horace hit her on the back and barked up at Ellie.

"I think she's choking," Dean said, and quick as lightning he picked Winkie up and gave her a hard squeeze. Nothing happened, so he did it again. Something happened this time—the bug shot out of Winkie's snout and the crystals shot out of her mouth. They landed on the stage a few

feet away from the jester.

It was quiet for a second, then everyone started hooting and clapping, as if Winkie was a part of the show or something. Humans were so weird.

At that point she didn't care what they did so long as she could breathe. She gulped air until Dean ran his hand over her head.

"Slow down, little one, or you'll make yourself sick."

Winkie forced herself to take normal breaths. Dean handed her over to Ellie, who held her close.

"Thank you, Dean!"

Horace hopped up on the bench beside them.

"Are you okay?" he asked.

She nodded. "Yeah. My throat hurts, but it's not too bad."

"I was so scared." His voice was rough like it got when he was trying not to be emotional.

"It would take more than a couple of stones to take this piglet out." She smiled at him.

His expression changed. "You were chewing rocks again?" he sputtered. "How many times do I have to tell you that it isn't safe?"

"Yes." She rolled her eyes. "But it wasn't rocks, it was crystals. I was sucking on them to heal the injury you gave me earlier. Where are my crystals now anyway?"

Horace finally harrumphed and said, "On the stage. But I forbid you from reclaiming them."

That's what he thought. As soon as he wasn't looking she was going to go get them. Except someone got there first—a hand scooped them up before she could even move. Winkie couldn't tell

who had taken
them on account of
all the people walking in front
of the stage. It was probably just
someone clearing the props and stuff.

Dang it, those healing crystals had really been helping her too.

Without warning, Uta Hawken swooped down and landed on the railing in front of them. The humans stepped back in surprise.

"I must speak with you on an urgent matter. Meet me here at midnight."

7

The Iron Tongue of Midnight

Horace was fit to be tied. The temerity of that bird telling him what to do! Who did she think she was? He wasn't some nincompoop without a thought in his head. He was a proud Boston Terrier with urgent business of his own.

"We have a case," he said. "An important one. The case of keeping Eleanor safe."

Bunwinkle sat on the porch next to him, eating ice cubes out of a tub with her name written on the side. They'd come home right after that horrible incident at the play. Eleanor had insisted on it. After a thorough examination had shown Bunwinkle was fine, she'd given them treats and then headed off to do chores.

Horace watched her as she worked. She'd pulled her curly brown hair back into a ponytail and put on her grubbiest clothes. He didn't understand how anyone could enjoy working on a farm, but it clearly made Eleanor happy. She was grinning as though she'd just been given a gift.

"We have to go see Uta." Bunwinkle's voice broke into his thoughts.

"Why?"

She rolled her eyes, "Because we're pettectives and we help people."

He snorted.

"And because Ellie isn't going to stay here forever. She'll go back to the faire tomorrow. We have to solve this to keep her safe."

That brought a frown to his face. He hated to admit it, but she was right. Eleanor was a brave woman. She wouldn't let anyone intimidate her. So the only way to protect her was to find the culprits.

"And also because everything that's gone wrong has gone wrong at the faire. Uta lives there so she has to know more."

That was all true, and yet Horace sensed there

was more to it with Bunwinkle. It was as though she was looking for reasons to go back at night. As though she was looking for something . . . or someone. He turned to look at her. "You're trying to see Santa Claus, aren't you?"

She snatched up an ice cube from the bowl and chewed it loudly. "Hmm? What? Can't hear you with all this noise."

A few minutes later Dean drove into the driveway. He rolled down his window and lifted a flat white box. "I brought pizza."

Eleanor grinned at him. "That sounds great."

Dean parked, and as a group they went inside. Horace couldn't help but notice how happy Eleanor was when Dean was around. How much more she laughed.

It was just pizza. It's not like the human nuisance really did anything to *help*.

"Thank you for milking the goats for me today," Eleanor said, setting the pizza on the kitchen counter.

All right, so he'd helped with the goats.

"You're very welcome. Oh, I also fixed the top

of the chicken coop while I was out there."

And he'd repaired the coop. That didn't mean anything.

Eleanor's smile brightened. "What would I do without you?"

Those words made Horace's heart ache. She didn't need that human. She had *him*. He had always watched over her and kept her safe. He'd licked tears from her face when she was sad and laughed with her when she was happy. Well, not exactly laughed—chuckled more like. But he'd done it because he loved her.

"Horace?" Bunwinkle's voice sounded far away. "Horace, it's okay."

But it wasn't okay. He was losing Eleanor.

A sticky snout touched his cheek, drawing his attention away from the humans.

"Don't cry. Ellie still loves you."

Good heavens! Had he said all of that out loud? Based on the sympathetic look Bunwinkle was giving him, he must have. But surely he wasn't crying.

A tear fell on his paw.

"Ah-hem," he cleared his throat and sat up

straight. "I have no idea what you're talking about. I never cry." He turned his head and wiped the other side of his face. "My eyes are damp due to seasonal allergies."

"Allergies. Right." Bunwinkle nodded a little too vigorously to be convincing.

Jennie walked through the back door, saving him from further embarrassment.

"Ooo, that looks good." She sidled up to the pizza box. "I'm going to steal a few pieces and head back to my room to do some research for my podcast, if that's okay with you two?"

Dean nodded, and Eleanor laughed. "You can sit out here, you know."

"Nah, I've got some work to do." She put three slices of pizza on a plate and grabbed a soda from the fridge. "Hey, Horace, Winkie, come back with me."

Horace wouldn't have done it, but then Jennie said, "I have french fries in my room."

* * *

Jennie had turned the spare room into what could only be described as a disaster. The futon bed was unmade, empty cups dotted every flat surface, and clothes were strewn everywhere. There wasn't even a place for Horace and Bunwinkle to sit.

"Sorry about this, guys." She picked up the yellow dress she'd been given by the faire and tossed it over the antique mirror in the corner. It hit with a thunk.

"Shoot, I keep forgetting to take that back."

Horace waited to see if there were, in fact, fries here or if he'd been hoodwinked. Bunwinkle didn't wait to be invited. She hopped up on the bed and started rooting around.

"They're not in the bed," Jennie said. "They're right here." She pulled a small paper cup off her desk and looked inside. "Oh, there are only a few left."

A few wound up being a half dozen french fries apiece. Once they had gobbled them up, Bunwinkle curled up next to Jennie on the bed. Horace went to stand by the door. Eleanor and Dean had been alone long enough. Jennie didn't notice him because she was eating pizza and texting someone. Her laptop was open on the bed beside her.

"I know he's not telling me everything and I'll prove it," she muttered to herself.

He cleared his throat.

"Horace." Jennie set her phone down on the bedside table and smiled at him. "Come snuggle with us."

Not a chance.

She pulled a piece of cheese off her pizza and held it up for him. "I've got a yummy treat here for you."

How dare she use cheese to lure him away from protecting Eleanor? He'd show her. He'd eat that cheese and then come right back to the door.

Horace walked to Jennie's side, head held high. As he took the cheese from her fingertips, he got a good look at her computer screen.

He'd assumed she was watching something, but it appeared that she was actually going through pictures, and not just any pictures—mug shots. There were six of them on the screen.

"Hey, I want some cheese too." Bunwinkle put

her hooves on Jennie's leg, accidentally hitting the space bar on the laptop.

A new set of mug shots popped up. Jennie didn't notice, though. She was too busy pulling Horace into a hug and smothering him with kisses. It was terribly embarrassing, and he only allowed it for a few minutes.

When she was done, Jennie put him down on the bed and said, "That's better. Now, I'll go get another drink and maybe some of those popcorn balls Dean made, and we'll continue our party in here." She stood up and set the laptop back on the bed.

Horace got ready to follow her. The door wouldn't be open long, so he'd have to be fast.

"Horace, wait." Bunwinkle's voice stopped him. "Come look at this."

"What is it?" He

POLICE DEPARTMENT

STANLEY TRIBY

WANTED IN
DELAWARE,NORTH CAROLINA
TEXAS

BURGLARY

kept his eyes on the door.

"I recognize this mug shot."

"What?" He turned back to her, and Jennie used the moment to slip out of the room.

"Blast. Now I'll have to do it when she comes back in, which is much harder."

Bunwinkle snorted. "Will you forget about getting out of here and look at this?"

Grudgingly he came back to the bed. "Which one do you recognize?"

"Top right corner." She pointed with her snout.

The picture showed a man with thick glasses, a scruffy beard, a receding hairline, and a large heart-shaped birthmark on the top of his forehead.

"It's the jester."

"I don't think so," he answered.

"It *is* him." Bunwinkle stomped her hoof, which didn't have the same effect, as they were still sitting on Jennie's bed. "I saw that birthmark on his forehead when Mr. O tried to pull his hat off."

Horace tilted his head. "But it doesn't look anything like him."

"That's because this is a really old picture. If

you take away the beard and the glasses and you put white face paint on him . . ."

Good heavens! She was right, it *was* the bell-wearing fool. Horace could see it now.

Underneath the picture, it read, "Stanley Triby, aka the King of Hearts. Wanted in Delaware, North Carolina, and Texas."

The screen suddenly flashed an empty battery sign, then went dark.

Horace shook his head. "I guess we *will* be going back to the faire tonight."

A few hours later, they were walking up Farthingale Fashion Drive. Without humans around, the faire had an eerie feeling to it, as though someone was hiding in the shadows waiting to jump out. Horace's sniffer twitched. Someone was nearby.

"Oh, hey, man. Didn't expect to see you two here."

Shoo stepped out from behind a trash bin, half a pickle in one hand and a beet in the other.

Bunwinkle squealed and leaped in the air. As she did her back hoof hit the beet and sent it flying straight up. It landed with a thunk on Shoo's head a moment later. The raccoon looked up as if he expected it to continue raining beets. When it became clear there wouldn't be any more, he bent down and picked it up.

"Will you look at that? I lost a beet and then a beet showed up. Gnarly, huh?"

It was definitely something.

Bunwinkle collected herself and stood up. "Shoo! What are you doing here?"

"Yes," Horace couldn't help adding, "I thought you had given up eating trash."

Shoo nodded. "Yeah, I'd appreciate if you wouldn't tell the princess about this. She thinks trash food is for . . . what was the word she used again? Pool noodles? Hoodies?"

"Hooligans?" Horace suggested.

"That's the one." The raccoon took a bite of the pickle and chewed with his mouth open. "She just doesn't understand there are certain delicacies you can only get at a special event like this." He took another bite of pickle and bits of partially chewed food fell out of his mouth. "I mean, look at these pickles. Where else are you gonna find a turkey-infused dill pickle?"

"Nowhere," Bunwinkle said.

"Thank goodness," Horace muttered to himself.

There was a clang off to the left, and again Bunwinkle squealed and jumped.

"Shoobert?"

It was Princess Sofaneesba.

A moment later the white cat emerged from the darkness, a worried expression on her face.

"Are you all right, Bunwinkle?" she asked the piglet sprawled at Horace's feet.

"Awesome."

Horace frowned at her. "Good heavens, what's gotten into you?"

"I'm just a little nervous about running into"— she glanced at the others, then leaned close to Horace and whispered—"you know who."

Horace stopped. His sniffer tingled and it brought the hair up on his back. They were in the presence of evil. He could feel it in his soul.

"What mischief is this?" a voice said.

The bird was back.

"As if we would make mischief. We're proper, well-behaved animals." Horace had no sooner said the words than Shoo sneezed, spraying the group with chunks of pickle.

"Ew, gross," Bunwinkle said.

Princess Sofaneesba had a different reaction. "Shoobert, have you been eating trash again?"

"No." Shoo panicked, and the next thing Horace knew a pickle collided with the side of his head.

The bird looked down her beak at them, and Horace was certain he heard her laugh.

"Yes, very proper," Hawken sneered.

"What do you want, fowl?"

She narrowed her eyes at him as if she were trying to decide whether to speak. With a heavy sigh she flew down beside Shoo.

The raccoon's eyes grew round. "Whoa. Did you guys know there was a bird here?" He looked around. "Is the guy with her too?"

Hawken squawked. "His name is Ted the Astringer."

Shoo nodded. "Can he do a personal horoscope for me? I'm a Libra and I've been feeling off ever since Mercury went into retrograde."

"Ooo," Princess Sofaneesba said, ears twitching in excitement. "I'd like one too. I'm a Sagittarius."

"That's astrology." Bunwinkle rolled her eyes. "Uta's human studies stars and planets and other outer space stuff."

"That's an astronomer. This man is an astringer," Horace informed them. "Astringers work with hawks. Just as falconers work with falcons."

They all nodded as though they understood, and then a moment later Shoo raised his hand.

"I would have called them hawkers, if it was up to me. Otherwise, people might get confused and think they worked with ostriches."

Horace glanced at Uta. She held a wing up to the side of her head as if she had a headache. For the briefest of moments Horace felt a connection with the bird. This group could drive even the most patient animal to distraction.

The sympathy lasted until he heard the bird mutter, "'More of your conversation would infect my brain.' That's from *Coriolanus*, act 2, scene 1."

How dare she insult Horace's friends! Only he could do that.

"To paraphrase that great New Englander, John Adams, you are 'one continued insult to good manners and to decency.'"

Uta lashed out with her wing. "Now you listen here, you insignificant—"

"Whoa, this situation is getting heavy," Shoo said, stepping between them. "Let's all take a deep breath and let go of our hostilities."

"I am never hostile." The hawk sniffed. "Why, I'm known for my pleasant demeanor. Sir Ian commended me for it when we worked on *A Midsummer Night's Dream*. He was delightful as Bottom. You should have seen him when he turned into a donkey."

Shoo, Princess Sofaneesba, and Bunwinkle looked at each other, confusion clear on their faces, then one by one a hand, a paw, and a hoof went into the air.

Oh no. If they started asking questions they'd be there all night, and Horace was already tired. It was time to get to the point.

"Enough of this," Horace said. "Bunwinkle and I are pet-tectives, and we're here to keep our human safe."

Out of the corner of his eye he noticed the other three lower their limbs. Good. Hopefully they'd forget all about the donkey bottom she'd spoken of earlier.

Bunwinkle stepped forward, her brow furrowed in earnestness. "That's right. You said you had something to tell us?"

Her demeanor would have been more impressive if there hadn't been a chunk of pickle stuck to the side of her face.

Uta leaned close, a wing held to her chest in a dramatic pose, as though she was acting a part in a play. "It started about a month ago. Ted let all our regular actors go and hired a whole new group. Then the location switched from our usual site to . . . this place. And we've had nothing but problems since we arrived. Horses go missing and are returned the next morning. Stalls are vandalized.

"Then today there was that play. Usually we use one script for the whole season. Ted writes them during the winter. But he did *not* write what we saw today. When he asked the actors about it, they all said the same thing. They'd received a script several days ago with a note to learn their parts. They had one rehearsal where they figured out the blocking themselves, and then they performed it."

"And no one knew who wrote it?" Horace asked.

The hawk shook her head. "No."

"Well, whoever wrote it wasn't very good,"

Bunwinkle said. "None of it made any sense."

Princess Sofaneesba purred. "Not to us. But I had the feeling it made sense to the jester."

Something was tickling at the back of Horace's mind. "Did you say horses had gone missing?"

"Yes."

"Which ones?" Bunwinkle asked.

"Actually, they were yours," Uta said with a frown.

"We need to talk to Smith and Jones," Horace said.

Horace would have preferred to limit the number of pet-tectives to two—himself and Bunwinkle—but it appeared he didn't have a choice. Shoo and the princess simply followed along when they started walking toward the horse stalls, and the Hawken creature said she'd meet them there.

Bunwinkle was quiet on the way.

"Are you all right?" he asked.

"Rah."

He sighed. "Are you chewing on rocks again?"

"No," she snorted. "I'm eating a pickle."

"Not the one Shoo threw on the ground?"

There was no answer, which told him everything he needed to know.

"Bunwinkle!"

Horace was so horrified he didn't hear the hawk until she landed next to him.

"We have a problem."

Oh no, what now?

"Hey, the horses are gone," Shoo said.

8

Blue Shoes Clues

Winkie squeezed her eyes shut and shook her head. The horses *had* to be there. But when she opened her eyes again, their stalls were still empty.

"Where could they have gone?" Princess Sofaneesba asked.

"I suggest . . . ," Horace and Uta said at the same time. They looked at each other as if they were waiting for the other one to go first. Then they talked together again. "We split up . . ." Another pause, another suspicious look, then really fast Horace said, ". . . and search for them."

He got a smug smile on his face like he'd won something.

And he said Winkie was immature! At least

she didn't get into speed-talking competitions.

"Whoa! Are you two, like, twins or something?" Shoo stared at them and scratched his head.

"No!" they snapped.

Winkie pressed her lips together real hard but a giggle got out anyway. She couldn't help it.

"Splitting up sounds like a lovely idea," the princess said. "We will search the south side of the faire and then meet back here." She nudged the raccoon with her nose. "Come along, Shoobert."

He nodded. "The energy is real weird around here."

As they walked away, Uta clicked her beak and said, "I shall take to the air, where I will be able to see all and sundry." Without waiting for them to say anything, she flew up and away.

"That is the rudest creature I have ever met," Horace huffed. "Did you see the way she behaved? Though what else would you expect from a feathered miscreant?"

Winkie waited for Horace to finish, but he just kept going. This was probably the most he'd ever talked. Ever. He didn't even talk about New

England this much. After a few minutes she stopped listening.

Maybe they were thinking of this wrong. Maybe they shouldn't go looking for the horses, maybe they should look for the jester.

"And the feathers . . ." Horace droned on.

"Yeah, feathers are the worst."

But where would he be? Probably in the tent area in the back.

Horace's voice interrupted her thoughts. "Don't even get me started on the talons."

"Yeah, talons are the worst."

"Where are you going?" Horace blocked the path in front of her.

"I'm going to look for the jester." She walked around him.

"Yes, excellent idea." Horace went on, "We have to put our full effort into this investigation. It's critical that we solve this case before . . . well, it's simply important to solve it as soon as possible."

"Yeah, and it would go a lot faster if you stopped complaining about birds and paid attention," Winkie said. "I thought you wanted to solve this mystery so nothing bad would happen to Ellie."

"Of course I do." Horace tilted his nose up. "And I can assure you that I am fully focused."

"Then let's get to work."

As they walked through the faire, Winkie's thoughts started going at superspeed.

"What do you think the jester is up to?"

"I wish I knew," Horace said. "The computer cut out before we could see what he was wanted for."

Another question popped into her brain. "How does Wendell fit into all this?"

Horace sighed. "Perhaps they're working together. We'll ask the horses when we find them."

They ran into trouble at the backstage area. The problem was the big sign saying STAFF ONLY. Winkie had already been back there, but Horace refused to go.

"It's forbidden," he said for the third time.

She rolled her eyes. "Forbidden? It's not a cursed tomb or something. It's just the unfancy part of the faire."

"We're not allowed back there," he insisted.

"That sign's for humans. When the faire is

open." She waved her snout around and said, "But it's closed now and there are no humans around. So let's go."

He pressed his lips together and sat down. "It's against the rules."

Oh, not this again. Horace had a thing about being a "good boy," and that meant he always followed the rules. Although Winkie noticed he wasn't so obedient when he broke the rule about licking his legs.

"Well, I'm going," she said and walked under the rope holding the sign.

Four steps in, Horace whispered in her ear, "This will end badly. I can feel it."

Winkie didn't say anything, but she secretly agreed.

"How long have we been out here?" Winkie asked after the third dead end.

"I don't know, but we're never going to find the jester, or the horses for that matter, like this."

"There has to be a way," Winkie said. "We're pet-tectives—we've solved two mysteries already. We found all those animals when they went missing, right?"

Horace shook his head. "Let's be honest, we didn't capture those culprits so much as stumble upon them accidentally."

"True, but—"

Winkie was cut off by the sound of someone stomping up the path talking to themselves.

"Quick, in here!" Horace grabbed her by the

neck and tossed her into a nearby tent.

That was the second time he had done that. They were going to have a very serious conversation about it when they got home.

"I swear, those horses are dumber than a box of hammers." The man stopped right outside the tent. "Dang it, which one of these tents is mine?"

Please don't let it be this one.

"Here it is. If it had been a snake it would have bit me." He walked past them and turned on a lantern.

"This way," Horace whispered as he shoved Winkie underneath a big cot with sleeping bags piled on it.

There wasn't much room to move around under there, especially when Horace joined her.

"This isn't going to work," she whisper-shouted at him.

Horace shook his head and pressed his lips together, which she guessed was his way of telling her to be quiet.

They could hear the man moving around, but it was hard to tell where he was in the tent. How were they going to get out of there if they didn't know when the coast was clear? They couldn't stay there all night.

"At this rate I'll never find those darn canaries."

Wait, that was the second time canaries had come up. Were these guys really looking for birds?

Something rustled above them.

What was that?

It turned out it was the sleeping bags getting moved so that someone could sit down. Winkie figured it out when the cot caved super low and she had to lie flat on her tummy to avoid getting squished.

Could this get any worse?

There were more creaks and rustling from above

that sounded as if the guy was stretching out.

"Never should have taken those diamonds. He said they were cursed. Only thing he ever got right."

Diamonds?

Winkie checked to see if Horace had heard, but he was too busy licking his legs and whispering, "Who's a good boy? You're a good boy!" to himself over and over.

Luckily the diamond guy fell asleep pretty quickly after that.

When he started snoring, Winkie whispered, "Time to go." She tripped over a muddy pair of blue shoes on her way out and got dirt in her mouth.

Yuck.

"I told you something terrible would happen if we broke the rules," Horace said once they were outside the tent.

"You were right," she said, spitting out dirt. "Now let's get out of here before someone else comes."

The others were all waiting at the meeting spot when they came running up.

"Oh, thank goodness," Princess Sofaneesba said when she saw them. "We were getting worried."

Horace put a paw to his chest. "We've been through a terrible ordeal."

"Like when the lemur captured you and threw you in the kennel?" Shoo asked.

Winkie shook her head. "No, but it was still scary."

The princess sighed. "It was like when the twins petnapped us, wasn't it?"

"Well, perhaps 'ordeal' was the wrong word," Horace said. "It was more of an inconvenience."

Uta watched all this with one raised eyebrow. "Nothing you creatures say makes sense."

Horace sat up straight and sniffed. They were gonna start fighting again if Winkie didn't do something.

"Did you find the horses?" she asked a little too loudly.

Finally, Uta stopped glaring at Horace and answered. "In a manner of speaking."

Winkie scrunched up her nose. What was that supposed to mean?

Uta flew down the path and landed on a corner post of the horse stalls. Three feet to her left was Smith. He was sound asleep with a smile on his face. Next to him stood Jones, humming "Jingle Bells."

"Where did you find them?" Winkie ran over to his stall.

"Standing right there," Uta said. "The culprits must have brought them back while we were out searching."

"Well, let's wake them up and ask them some questions," Horace said.

Shoo shook his head. "Can't. They're in some kind of trance."

Horace pressed his lips together the way he did when he got impatient. "Trance? Really?"

"Watch." Shoo scrambled up the wooden fence

and leaned close to Jones's ear. "HEY! WAKE
UP!"

Every one of them jumped except the horses.

Horace sighed. "I suppose we can speak with
them tomorrow."

"Yes," Uta agreed. "But it would be best to share our information now, while it's fresh in our minds."

"At first, we found nothing," Shoo said. "It was dark and quiet like you'd expect it to be. Then we saw a flash of red and heard someone speaking Italian."

"Italian? Are you sure?" Horace asked.

Shoo nodded as he climbed back down. "Oh yeah, I spent some time in Venice and I recognized it. The guy was talking about some kind of cookbook. He said *ricettario*, the Italian word for *cookbook*, several times. Maybe he was going to cook dinner for someone."

Princess Sofaneesba put a paw on his arm. "Actually, I think he may have said *ricettatore*."

"Huh," Shoo looked more confused than usual. "Why would he want a fence?"

"I don't get it," Winkie said. "Why would some random guy be here at night in a red suit speaking a foreign language? Unless . . ."

Horace bumped her side, "It wasn't Santa Claus."

"Right. Totally. 'Cause Jones was just confused

and a guy wearing a red suit isn't automatically Santa, right?"

Uta shook her head at Winkie, then focused on Shoo again. "What else did he say?"

"He got another call and then he started using a different kind of language, if you get my drift." Shoo gave them a knowing glance.

"I don't—" Winkie started but Horace put up a paw to stop her.

"He was swearing."

"Oooohhh."

"After that he hung up his phone and ran off to the tent area behind the stage. The one that's off-limits."

"Did you follow him?" Uta asked.

The princess answered this time. "Unfortunately, Shoobert became ill and we had to attend to that. By the time he recovered, the man was gone."

"Besides," Shoo added, "it's against the rules to go back there unless you work at the faire, and I didn't want to get in trouble."

Horace cleared his throat loudly. "I wonder who else said that?"

Winkie ignored him. "Hey, I think we saw that guy."

She told them all about the tents and almost getting caught, but for some reason she didn't mention the jester.

"A cookbook, a fence, and diamonds," Uta said. "That doesn't make any sense."

"What about you, Hawken?" Horace asked. "What did you learn?"

She sat up tall. "I discovered a white truck hidden behind a row of shrubs on the far northwest side of the faire. The back was full of your wooden buckets." She paused and looked away, then went on, "Perhaps that's what the villains were after in the first place. They're quite valuable, I understand."

That wasn't right, though. Winkie had seen that truck the day before and there had only been one bucket in it. And the jester had sworn he hadn't taken it. Of course, he was a criminal so he might lie about it, but it really felt like Uta was the one lying.

"So we have two missing horses who magically returned while we were searching for them, a man in a red suit speaking Italian about either a cookbook or a fence, and a truck full of Nantucket buckets." Horace sighed. "What is going on at this faire?"

Winkie stared at Uta. What *was* going on?

9

Out of Court

Horace was perplexed. There were so many pieces to this mystery, but none of them seemed to go together. Of one thing he was certain: this was about far more than a half dozen wooden buckets.

Unsurprisingly, Shoo and the princess didn't question Hawken's suggestion that the thieves were after Eleanor's buckets. They weren't privy to all the information that he and Bunwinkle had. Speaking of his sister pig, she'd become awfully quiet since the bird had shared her information.

"Are you all right?" he asked her.

She nodded. "Just thinking." She stopped and the others stopped as well. "Hey, Shoo, you've been roaming around at night, right?"

He looked at the white cat next to him, then back at Bunwinkle. "Yeah. I've been communing with nature and soaking up the moon rays."

Most likely he'd been rooting around for trash.

"Have you seen anything weird since the faire started?"

Why hadn't she asked Horace that question? He was out here every night making sure she and Eleanor were safe.

Shoo scratched his head. "No . . . Well, except for that night I found the healing crystals in the field."

"When was that?" Bunwinkle asked. Her face was more serious than Horace had ever seen it.

"Uh," Shoo moved from scratching the top of his head to scratching his chin. "That's kind of a problem. See, I don't really believe in time. I'm more about living in the moment."

Princess Sofaneesba smiled and patted his arm. "It was a few nights after the faire started. The night of the new moon, I believe."

"That's my lady, she knows everything."

Bunwinkle wrinkled her snout at them, but she didn't drop the matter.

"And they were just sitting out there all by themselves?" she pressed.

All of a sudden Shoo started fidgeting and looking at his feet. "Yeah. They were just sitting on the ground. I definitely did *not* touch a dude's ankle and scare him so bad he screamed and threw the bag of crystals at my head."

Silence followed that statement, and then the princess whispered, "Shoobert."

The raccoon turned to her and dropped to his knees. "I'm sorry. I didn't mean to scare anyone, but these two dudes were fighting real loud and

I figured they just needed a hug. I didn't expect them to get violent. Besides, I thought the bag had treats in it. Please don't tell my mom."

"But you kept the bag that clearly didn't belong to you," Horace pointed out.

"Well, yeah. They ran off and I didn't know who they were so I just sorta kept them. Finders keepers, ya know."

Bunwinkle frowned. "And there were definitely two men?"

Shoo nodded.

"Was one of them wearing a red suit?"

Was she talking about Wendell now or Santa Claus?

"It was kinda hard to tell in the dark. I just remember the guy with the white face paint because I thought he was a ghost at first."

Horace bumped her with his shoulder. "It's definitely the jester, then."

"Yeah, but who's he working with?" Bunwinkle asked worriedly.

When the alarm went off the following morning, Horace groaned and buried his head under a blanket.

He and Bunwinkle had finally crept into the house sometime after 3:00 a.m. Bunwinkle was silent the entire time. He'd tried to talk to her, but she'd simply said, "In the morning."

Now his eyelids felt as though they were made of sandpaper and his brain had turned to oatmeal. And most irritating of all was the fact that Bunwinkle did not appear to be having the same issues. She'd been moving around since the sun came up, and now she was standing next to his bed with her snout in his ear.

"I need to talk to you." She probably meant it as a whisper, but that close her voice was loud enough to make him jump.

He pulled his head from under his covers. "Not yet. My brain isn't ready to work yet."

She bumped him with her side. "You need to do some yoga to wake up. Let's try downward dog."

"I'm doing it right now. I am a dog and I am down."

"Come on. You need to pay attention. This is important."

Horace sighed and forced himself to focus. "What's going on?"

"Uta tried to trick us last night. She said there were a bunch of buckets in the back of a white truck, but that isn't true. I saw that truck, and there was only one bucket. I think she wanted to steer us in the wrong direction."

"I knew it." He sat upright. "What do I always say? Never trust a bird."

Bunwinkle disappeared for a second, then reappeared pushing Jennie's laptop across the floor.

"She's going to be upset if you damage her computer," Horace said.

"It's fine. Those dents were already there," Bunwinkle assured him before using her front teeth to lift the lid.

"Was the drool there as well?"

She stuck her tongue out at him as she typed something into the computer.

"Isn't it password protected?" he asked.

"Yeah. But I figured it had to be something she loved so I typed in 'french fries' and it worked."

She tapped a few more keys, then turned the laptop around for him to see. "I looked up the jester again. Stanley Triby used to be part of a crew that robbed jewelry stores, then he got caught and went to jail. That's where that mug shot came from. The thing is, after he got out, he disappeared. The police have been looking for him ever since."

"And you think he's hiding out at this ridiculous Renaissance Faire?"

She grinned at him. "I think he's doing a lot more than hiding out. I think he's the head of the Horse Apple Gang."

Horace stood and stretched to help get his brain moving. "Isn't that the group Jennie told Eleanor about?"

Bunwinkle nodded. "Yeah. They're kind of a big deal. They've been stealing for ten years, which is about when Triby got out of jail. They've pulled off jobs all over the country—Delaware, North Carolina, Texas—and never been caught."

"Why would he attach himself to something like the faire, where he'd be seen every day?'

"Well, he wears makeup and that outfit so you can't really tell what he looks like. Besides, I think his accomplices are also at the faire."

"Accomplices?" Horace's head was spinning. "You think he has more than one?"

"Obviously Wendell is working with him, but I'm pretty sure Ted is too." Bunwinkle looked sad as she told him.

It couldn't be true. Ted had always been nice and helpful, even though he kept a bird as a pet.

Without a word, Bunwinkle hit a key on the laptop and the faire's website came up, showing a map of all the places they'd toured in Delaware, North Carolina, and Texas.

Horace looked at his sister. "That doesn't seem like a coincidence."

"I don't think it is. I saw Ted talking to the jester a couple days ago and he said something like he didn't want his legal business to get in trouble. That sounds like he's got *illegal* business too. Right? Probably with the jester and Wendell. And I think Uta lied about the truck to protect Ted."

He could understand the urge to protect one's human. He would have done it for Eleanor. But, of course, she would never be involved with anything criminal, so he wouldn't have to.

"The robbery Jennie was talking about—it was in this area. They must have taken Smith and Jones to pull it off. What was the name of the person they robbed?"

"Howard?" Bunwinkle suggested, then shook her head. "No, that's not it. It started with an *H*, I think."

"Hewel! It was Mildred Hewel's estate."

"Let's look it up and see what else we can find," Bunwinkle said.

The first article went over the details they

144

already knew, but the second one was a wealth of information.

AN INTERVIEW WITH MILDRED HEWEL

I'd gone to the opera to see *Madame Butterfly*, but got bored so I decided to leave. If you've seen one soprano die on stage, you've seen them all. Anyway, I pulled into my driveway and what did I see? Horses! I knew something was wrong right away. We haven't kept horses since I was a little girl. I called the police then I stopped at the garden shed to get my BB gun. It was fully loaded and ready to go. I wasn't going to take a chance on anyone getting away with my property.

Those fools didn't know what hit them. They ran like a bunch of chickens. Got away with some of my best jewelry, though. And, of course, the canaries my husband gave me when we got married.

Horace looked up at Bunwinkle. "Why does this all sound familiar?"

Her eyes lit up. "It's the play! This is the same story from the court play!"

Good heavens!

Something bothered him about that story, though. "You know what doesn't make sense to me? Why would anyone steal canaries? They're birds. How valuable could they be?"

Bunwinkle's forehead wrinkled up like she was thinking hard. She switched internet tabs and looked up expensive canaries. It took a while to type with her snout, but eventually she did and a page full of pictures popped up. At the bottom of the page there was a photo showing a pile of shiny yellow rocks.

"Shoo's healing crystals!"

A glint of excitement filled her eyes. "Not crystals. Diamonds. Unrefined *canary* diamonds, to be precise."

Horace felt a rush of exhilaration. "It's all starting to make sense. I wondered why they took the horses and got mud in the buckets. They were digging for the diamonds. Although, I confess, I still don't understand why they destroyed all those stalls at the faire."

"Maybe they were looking for the diamonds."

"But why write 'Time to Pay' on the stalls?

That sounds like someone was after more than precious gems to me," Horace said.

Jennie walked into the room, looking like she'd just rolled out of bed. She stopped when she saw them. "Is that my laptop?"

"Do you think Jennie's figured all this out?" he asked Bunwinkle.

She wrinkled her snout and tilted her head. "I'm not sure, but I think she might have. She had a lot of notes in her computer that I couldn't read. I think they were in some kind of code."

Horace sighed. "We're going to have to watch over her."

Eleanor came in a minute later dressed for ice-cream making.

"You're going back?" Jennie asked.

"Yeah." Eleanor pulled her hair back in a pony-tail. "No one is going to intimidate me."

"We have to find the third thief before things get more dangerous," Horace whispered.

Wendell was waiting for them when they arrived at the stall. Horace immediately went on high alert—ears up, teeth bared. Bunwinkle did the same thing next to him, and though it didn't look terribly intimidating, Horace appreciated the effort.

"I heard someone wrecked your stall." His voice was steady and calm, with a hint of menace. This was the first time Horace actually believed the young man could be a real threat.

"We weren't the only ones." Eleanor nodded at the scone shop. "But, as you can see, we're not giving up."

"Maybe you should," he said without looking at her. "Might be safer."

"Hey, that sounded like a threat!" Bunwinkle said before making a weird gurgling noise in her throat.

"What are you doing?" Horace asked, careful not to take his eyes off Wendell.

"Growling. Does it sound impressive?"

Horace paused. "Well, it's definitely concerning."

"What are you doing here?" Clary asked, walking into the tent.

"Checking on the piglet. She choked on something at the play the other day, didn't she?" He squatted in front of Bunwinkle and ran a hand down her back.

There was something calculating in his eyes that made Horace uncomfortable. Based on the increased volume of her gurgling, Bunwinkle must have felt it as well.

"She's good now," Eleanor said. "She has a bad habit of chewing rocks. I've tried to give her other things to chew on, but she always manages to find something she shouldn't eat, especially here at the faire."

"Does she now?" Wendell stared at Bunwinkle, an odd little smile on his face. "What a naughty little pig you are."

Bunwinkle glanced at Horace and they both shivered.

A few minutes later Wendell went on his way. As soon as he was out of sight, Bunwinkle collapsed against Horace's side.

"That was the creepiest thing that's ever happened to me—and I've been pignapped."

Before they could discuss it further, another guest arrived at their tent.

"Knock, knock."

The king stood a few feet away from them. He wore his fine red outfit and a big grin, and he had a wooden bucket in each hand. "I wanted to apologize about the damage to your stall and the theft of your items. I don't know why anyone would do such a thing."

"Thanks," Eleanor said. "We appreciate that."

"And I wanted to offer you the use of these buckets for the duration of the faire."

Clary smiled as she took them from him. "Thank you so much." She held them up for Eleanor to see. "They're Nantuckets!"

"And how is that adorable little piglet of yours? She had quite a fit the other day. I was worried for her."

He bent down and tapped Bunwinkle's snout. Oh, big mistake. Bunwinkle hated it when humans did that.

Eleanor's forehead wrinkled. "That's funny. I was just talking with the Merchant of Vegetables about the same thing. Bunwinkle's fine. And I don't think she'll be chewing on any more rocks after that experience."

"Like to dig around for rocks, do you, little

one?" The king bent down as if he was going to touch Bunwinkle's snout again, but then she snapped at him and he pulled his hand back.

"If he does that again, I'm really gonna bite him."

The man seemed to understand her because he backed away with an uneasy smile. "Well, good luck with everything. I hope the buckets help."

He waved at them, then practically ran away.

"That was peculiar," Horace said.

"Yeah," Bunwinkle agreed. "But at least we didn't have to deal with the jester."

Bunwinkle's reply was drowned out by the jingle jangle of bells and the strum of a lute.

"A song for yon pig."

10

To Do a Great Right, Do a Little Wrong

Had anyone ever died from embarrassment? Because Winkie was pretty sure she was about to. The jester had set up a mini stage three feet from their stall and was performing a song he called "The Horking Pig."

"What piglet is this that throws such fits?" he sang.

"Doesn't he know any other tune than 'Greensleeves'?" Horace's lip curled up in disgust.

She stared at her brother. "He's singing a song about how I barf up rocks and you're bothered by the melody?"

"Fair point."

The jester continued his song. "She horks up rocks. She horks up socks—"

Hey! That wasn't true. She'd never even chewed on a sock. They didn't feel right in her mouth.

Seven verses later, Winkie was spitting mad. "We're never going to be able to investigate with him around."

Horace didn't hear her on account of him having

his paws over his ears. After the second verse, he'd dropped to the ground and covered them.

"Next verse," the jester sang.

"Enough." Ellie looked about as angry as Winkie. "You're driving customers away. The song was funny for the first verse, but now it's annoying."

"You wound me." He held a hand to his chest.

Ellie glared at him. "Not yet, but if you keep singing I will."

A normal person would have packed up and left, but not this guy. He just smiled and said, "Is that any way to treat someone who brought you a gift? Check the wheelbarrow on the other side of your stall."

Clary peeked around the side of the tent. "Buckets."

"That's correct," the jester nodded, and his bells jingled. "Heard you ladies were vandalized, and I wanted to help."

Ellie gave him a funny look. "Thanks. And my piglet is just fine. She won't be coughing up any more rocks at your play."

The jester hopped to his feet, jingling and

jangling all over the place. "How did you know I was going to ask?"

Winkie bumped Horace with her side. "It's safe now. He's stopped singing."

Horace sat up. "Good heavens, I thought it would never end."

"I'll be off, then." The jester bowed to Ellie, then he bowed to Winkie and whispered, "Be careful, little pig. You don't want to chew any more rocks, you hear me?"

"I think we should follow him." Winkie got to her hooves.

Horace held up a paw. "Wait. I'm not sure that's a good idea—I don't think it's safe. We had three visitors today and all three of them menaced you."

He was right. It probably wasn't safe. That had never mattered to her before, but after getting pignapped once and held hostage another time, she had discovered it did matter.

"So what are we gonna do?" she asked.

"We're going to stick close to Eleanor, and then when we get home we're going to find a way to contact the police."

And that is exactly what they did. Good thing

too. Because Wendell, the king, and the jester all passed by the stall again a bunch of times. Even Ted came by. Winkie noticed Uta wasn't with him.

Winkie didn't relax until they were at home that night. Ellie put peanut butter in her tube toy and she gnawed on it until she felt like she could think again. She knew Horace was upset too because he licked his legs for a long time.

As they were getting into bed Winkie brought up the police again. "How are we going to tell the police what's going on here? We can't exactly call them."

"We'll send an email first thing tomorrow," Horace said.

Unfortunately, there wasn't time to send an email. They all slept late and wound up rushing to get to the stall before the faire opened. By the time they got there, the jester had set up his stage in the dining area across from their stall. Winkie clenched her jaw when he started to sing.

By afternoon she had a headache the size of Godzilla. "I can't take it anymore. I want to go home."

"He's coming over again." Horace didn't have to say who—the jingling told Winkie everything she needed to know.

The jester stopped right in front of her. "How are those buckets working out?" he asked.

"They're great," Clary said for the third time that day. "Thank you again."

The king walked up at that moment. "Jester, why don't you leave these good people in peace. They've been through enough without having to listen to your music."

People laughed; a few even clapped. Winkie was so grateful she could have kissed the king's feet. She looked down at them, then gasped.

Blue shoes.

"Horace!" she whispered as loud as she dared. "His shoes!"

"What about them?"

She rolled her eyes. "They're the ones I tripped over in that tent. The night we met Uta and the horses went missing."

"Are you sure?" Horace asked as he stood up.

"Yes!" Winkie stared at the king's feet. Those were definitely the shoes. And Princess Sofaneesba had pointed them out at the tournament too. It all made sense, even the horses. "He's the guy Jones thought was Santa Claus."

"And he's the one in the video we saw."

Winkie couldn't believe it. Was everyone at this faire part of the Horse Apple Gang? It made her shiver just thinking about it.

"Stay calm," Horace whispered and pressed the side of his body against hers. "He's not going to do anything to us here, not in front of Eleanor and everyone. We're safe."

She leaned against him. "I guess we shouldn't be surprised. He's been coming by since the play yesterday too. He probably thinks I have the diamonds. And remember how he stopped Jennie from giving away that costume hanky with the pearls? I bet those were real pearls."

"Yes, and he got upset when he saw her in that yellow dress."

Winkie nodded. "The one that was lumpy and heavy and—"

"I know where the jewels are!" they said at the same time.

"We need to get back to the house as soon as

possible." Horace looked around frantically "And we're going to need help."

"Shoo and the princess will help. And it's almost time for the play, so we know exactly where they are." Winkie glanced around. The king had pulled the jester aside and they were talking close together now. Every once in a while, one of them would look over. "Now we just have to wait for them to go do the play and then we can go."

"We have to be careful not to let Hawken see us," Horace added. "She's not to be trusted."

A few minutes later both the king and the jester left. Winkie and Horace snuck out of the stall and made their way down to the tournament ring. Horace insisted they stick to the shadows, to mask their movements.

They were about to walk under the bleachers when a shadow flew over to them.

"What are you doing?" Uta's voice was so cold it made Winkie shiver.

"Nothing that concerns you," Horace answered.

"Actually, I believe it does. I'm afraid Ted has done something foolish. And it's up to me to fix it."

Horace stared at the hawk, then surprised

Winkie by saying, "I understand. Come along."

"Something's wrong," Shoo said as soon as he saw them.

Winkie stopped. "How did you know?"

He tapped the side of his head. "I can see your energics. They're all wild and messy." He nodded, then continued, "That, and I was getting a pastrami taco at the food stand next to you and I overheard everything."

Horace snorted.

Uta cleared her throat. "Before we go on, I feel I owe you an apology. I lied the other day when I mentioned the truck with the buckets. I was trying to protect Ted but I can see that it's no use."

Shoo raised his hand. "Hey, we know that truck. It's all covered in mud and stuff. We just saw the king over by it. He pulled out one of your fancy buckets."

The princess cut in. "And then he put several suitcases in the back."

Winkie turned to her brother. "He's making a run for it!"

Horace shook his head. "But he doesn't have the dress or the diamonds. You still have the bag of healing crystals, right, Shoo?"

Shoo looked down at his feet, up at the sky, anywhere but at his friends.

Princess Sofaneesba bumped his side. "Shoo?"

"About that. See, I went out for a stroll last night. Just to see the stars—not because I was eating garbage or anything—and I set it down so I could get"—he glanced at the princess—"a drink of water. But while I was getting . . . the water, someone pushed me into the compost bin. When I got out the bag was gone."

"So the king's got the diamonds," Horace said. "But not the rest of the jewels. He'll definitely go after them soon."

"What's the plan?" Shoo asked.

Horace immediately answered, "We're going to take down the king, the jester, Wendell, *and* Ted before they can get away. With four bad guys, it's going to take all of us to stop them, which means we're going to have to split up again. Uta, we need you to go backstage and keep your eyes on the culprits. You're part of the cast, so it won't look suspicious if anyone spots you. And if one of them tries to leave, give a loud cry."

"And what will you do?" the hawk asked.

"Shoo and the princess will stay here while Bunwinkle and I go around to the left side of the stage. Then when they're both onstage, we'll rush up and overtake them."

"It's a passable plan." Uta sniffed.

Horace smiled. "Thank you."

What was going on? Horace would never be that nice to a bird, especially not the hawk. Winkie frowned. He had to be up to something.

"Now, let's all go to our positions," he said.

Uta nodded and flew off. Horace took a few steps, then peeked up at the sky.

"Excellent, she's gone. Now I can share our real plan."

Winkie bounced up and down. "I knew it! I knew you would never be so polite to Uta."

"Yes, you know me well. I knew we'd never be able to pull this off if we had to hide from her."

Princess Sofaneesba said, "Very clever of you. Now what is the real plan?"

"Shoo and the princess, you go back to the truck and disable it. We're going to make it as hard as possible for him to get away."

Shoo looked confused. "Which truck is that again?"

"The one that's covered in muck," Horace answered. "The one the king put his bags in."

"Oh, right."

Horace looked at Winkie. "And we're going to back to the house for the dress."

"This is very exciting!" Princess Sofaneesba clapped her paws together.

A thought suddenly hit Winkie. "Hey, should

we go after the shoes?"

"No," Horace shook his head. "Mildred Hewel's diamonds are much more important."

"Don't you think finding the shoes would help prove the king was involved?"

Shoo smiled and waved. "I'm right here."

"Not you," Winkie waved her hoof at him. "The blue shoes."

"Nah, I don't wear shoes. They hurt my arches." Shoo lifted a foot and showed them the bottom of it. "I got real flat feet. See?"

"Yes, thank you, Shoo." Horace shook his head. "Bunwinkle, blue shoes won't help. What we need now are the jewels."

"So we're going to the house for the jewels that were Hewel's?" Winkie asked.

Horace nodded.

Shoo raised his hand. "Do I need shoes for this activity?"

"No. All you have to do is disable the truck covered in muck."

It was quiet for second. Not the silence of animals who understood, but a deeply confused silence.

"Let's go over it again," Horace said. "Bunwinkle

and I will search for the dress that's a mess and has the jewels that were Hewel's while Shoo and the princess sabotage the truck in the muck where the king put his things."

The trip back to the house was quick and quiet. The chicks didn't even react when they ran by.

Winkie hadn't thought it possible, but Jennie's room was even messier than the last time they were there.

"How are we going to search this?" she asked.

Horace shrugged. "I suppose we simply have to pick a place and start."

Winkie picked a pile of clothes next to the mirror.

"Aw, gross."

"You know, I adore Jennie, but she really is a dreadful slob."

"No kid—" Winkie stopped. She heard something.

"Mailman!" the chicks screamed. "Mailman!"

Winkie's heart raced. "Someone's coming."

"Hide!"

There wasn't time to be picky, which is how

they both wound up under the pile of dirty clothes.

"My sniffer can't handle this," Horace muttered.

"Stick out your muzzle. That'll help."

They cleared a little spot so they could breathe. It also gave them a view into the room. The door slowly opened, and the king slipped in. He glanced around, his nose wrinkling in disgust.

"Where is it? Where did she put that dress?" He opened the closet door and rifled through the clothes.

"What's going on, Louie?" The jester stood in the doorway.

The king went white, but he still managed to paste a phony smile on his face.

"I'm just here to get the dress. We've got to pay Otis Mayes before he comes after us again. Next time he'll do more than wreck a few stalls."

Winkie looked over at Horace and whispered, "So these guys didn't mess up the faire?" Horace shrugged. "I guess it was this Otis Mayes person."

Dang it. Why was that name so familiar? She'd heard it before. It hit her like lightning. Smith had said the name when he was sleep-talking, which made sense since he had been there when they went to Hewel's house.

"Right. And here I was thinking you were fixing to take the loot and hightail it out of here." The jester stepped into the room. He was bigger than King Louie, by a lot.

"Don't be silly, Stan." He laughed, but it sounded fake to Winkie, even with all the clothes piled on her.

The jester cracked his knuckles and walked up to his accomplice. "You know, you're a terrible liar. But it doesn't matter, because you're not going anywhere.

"Hey, El. Everything okay?" Dean's voice echoed through the house. "The front door was open so I thought I'd check on you."

The king used the distraction to his advantage. He reached into a pile of clothes and pulled out the yellow dress. "Got it!"

Dean peeked his head in just as King Louie opened the door. "El?"

Louie grabbed Dean's arm and swung him into Stan.

"He's going to run for it," Winkie said.

"We've got to stop him!" Horace said. "Let's go for the legs."

They sprang out of the dirty clothes pile and chased after Louie. Unfortunately, Winkie tripped over an empty soda can and went down, but Horace kept going. He leaped up and caught hold of the yellow dress just as the king was running away. Stan grabbed hold of it a second later. Now they were locked in a three-way tug of war. Louie stumbled to the side, hitting the mirror.

"Look out!" Winkie yelled.

11

All's Well That Ends Well

Horace froze. He tried to run, but his legs simply wouldn't move. He closed his eyes and braced for the impact. This was going to hurt a great deal.

Something did fall on him, but it wasn't hard and made of glass. It was a body. Dean's body. A few seconds later the mirror made contact, shaking both of them and drawing a groan from the human.

"No!" Bunwinkle squealed.

Horace stared up at Dean's face. The man's eyes were squeezed shut and his lips were clenched together in pain.

Dean had saved him. If that mirror had landed on Horace he would have been badly injured. He was certain of it.

While he was processing what had just happened someone shouted, "FBI! FREEZE!"

Huh, that sounded like Wendell. But that couldn't be right.

It *was* right. It turned out that Wendell, the Merchant of Vegetables, was actually Wendell Dryer, FBI agent. After he'd arrested Stan and Louie, he'd escorted Horace, Bunwinkle, and Dean out to the back porch so the FBI team could process Jennie's room.

"Good luck with that," Bunwinkle whispered as they sat down on the steps. She'd moved to Horace's side the moment Dean had uncovered him, and she'd stayed there ever since.

"How did you know they were here?" Dean asked the question that had been bothering Horace.

"Ted tipped us off." Wendell tilted his head toward the faire owner, who stood a few feet away talking to another FBI agent. Uta sat on his shoulder. As they looked over, she turned and nodded her head, but Horace was certain he heard her whisper "Cur" under her breath.

Wendell continued talking, unaware of the rudeness. "He came to us when Stan and Louie contacted him again. I can't imagine how long it would have taken us to nab them if he hadn't."

Jennie walked up as he finished talking. "That was smart of him. He had to know they'd come back to the faire every time they ran out of money. Plus, it was the only way to get that loan shark, Otis Mayes, from destroying his life's work—the faire." She turned to Wendell and asked, "Does this mean Ted won't do any jail time?"

Wendell frowned. "We'll have to see about that.

He may not have been involved in this heist, but he definitely helped with others in the past."

"Oh, give him a break." Jennie bumped him with her shoulder. "He only did it to keep the faire running so his hawk would have a place to perform."

The frown deepened. "And how do you know that?"

"Because I interviewed him for my podcast." She grinned at Wendell. "Speaking of which, is now a good time for the interview you promised? You told me if I helped with the play, you'd give me full access."

The play. She was behind that. How sneaky of her to do that and not tell Eleanor!

"No, now isn't a good time. I'm still in the middle of wrapping this case up." Wendell turned away from her. "You'll just have to wait."

"I think they like each other," Bunwinkle said with a giggle.

Horace rolled his eyes but stayed silent. He couldn't think about that at the moment.

Finally, Wendell said, "I think that's all I have for you right now." He smiled and added, "There's someone who wants to see you." He held up his hand and someone came running over.

It was Eleanor, of course. She scooped up Horace and hugged him. "Oh, baby boy, you had me so worried." She held him a little bit longer, then set him down and picked up Bunwinkle. "You two have to stop doing this to me."

When she was finished inspecting them, she turned her attention to Dean. "Jennie told me what you did. Are you okay?"

"My back hurts," Dean said with a lopsided smile. "But I'll live."

She smiled back. "Stay put. I'll get some ice for you."

"We should go with her," Bunwinkle said.

Horace nodded and slowly got to his feet. He hadn't taken more than two steps when Dean held up his hand. "Why don't you sit with me for a bit, Horace?"

Normally Horace would have turned his nose up at the suggestion, but Dean had saved his life, so the least he could do was sit with the man. If Dean started to gloat, however, Horace would just have to leave him here.

"Go on without me," Horace called out to Bunwinkle.

"Actually, I'm going to see what those guys want." She pointed her snout at a pair of heads sticking out from behind a tent. Shoo and Princess Sofaneesba waved. Horace waved back, then returned to his spot by Dean.

He wondered what the man wanted to talk about.

Turns out nothing. They sat there quietly for what felt like a very long time.

Was Dean going to say anything? Horace could have been protecting Eleanor right now or helping Bunwinkle wrap up the case. Then Dean sighed. It was the saddest sigh Horace had ever heard.

"I know you don't think that much of me, Horace, and that's probably my fault. I'm sorry if it seems like I'm a threat. I don't mean to be."

Horace looked at Dean. An apology seemed like a good start.

Dean continued, "Can I tell you something? I haven't said this to anyone yet, but I like Eleanor. A lot. Maybe more than a lot."

Horace shifted uncomfortably. This wasn't the conversation he'd been expecting. It always made him uncomfortable when people talked about their feelings, but it was even worse hearing Dean's.

"She does such a great job of taking care of everyone, especially you and Bunwinkle."

Horace had to agree, Eleanor was wonderful.

"And I know you take care of her too. I've seen it." Dean ran a hand gently down Horace's back. "Eleanor, Bunwinkle, the goats, the horses, the ducks—well, maybe not the ducks—but you do a lot around here."

Horace felt a little lump in his throat.

"I've never had a pet before, so this is all new to me, but I'd like to help take care of everyone on the Homestead. Eleanor, Bunwinkle, the animals." Dean paused. "And you too, if you'll let me. I've come to care a lot about all of you."

Good heavens, now Horace's eyes felt damp. Probably just his allergies acting up again. He definitely wasn't moved by Dean's words.

"What do you say, Horace? Can we be friends?"

Friends? Horace waited for the old resentment to flare, but to his surprise, what he felt was relief. How nice it would be to have help protecting the ones he loved. Bunwinkle was a great sister, but she attracted trouble like flowers attracted bees. Sometimes the worry kept him awake at night.

And suddenly Horace understood. Dean wasn't trying to steal Eleanor. He simply wanted to be a part of their family. Horace thought about it. Was there room for someone else on the Homestead?

Dean moved his hand to scratch behind

Horace's ears. "You really are a good boy."

Perhaps he'd misjudged the man. After all, Dean had never had a pet before. Horace would just have to train him.

"I'm glad to see you two getting along so well." Eleanor reappeared with Bunwinkle at her side.

"Where does it hurt?" Eleanor said as she squatted down behind Dean.

He pointed to a spot near his shoulder, and she placed the ice pack on it. "Does that help?"

"Yeah." He turned his head and smiled at her. "Thank you."

"No, thank *you*. If you hadn't stepped in, we would have lost Horace. And Bunwinkle. You saved her too." She leaned forward and hugged Dean from behind.

What was this? Hugging? That was a bit too much.

Bunwinkle blocked Horace's path. "What happened between you two?"

"What do you mean?" Horace tried to look innocent and at the same time tried to peek around Bunwinkle to monitor the hug situation.

"Give me a break," she snorted. "I was gone for

five minutes and you guys suddenly became best friends."

"Friendly, that's all. I only have one best friend, and that's you."

She turned pink and grinned at him. "You're my best friend too."

Out of the corner of his eye Horace could see Eleanor and Dean still hugging. His irritation levels rose. He was going to have to do something drastic to take his mind off it.

"You know, I think I'm ready to learn yoga."

A Note from the Author

Thank you so much for reading *Horace & Bunwinkle: The Case of the Fishy Faire*. If you're like me, you've fallen in love with Boston Terriers and potbellied pigs. But before you go rushing off to buy one, there are some important things you should know.

First, there's no such thing as Teacup pigs or Pixie pigs or pigs that stay small. All pigs get big, like 100–200 pounds big. Yeah, that's small compared to farm hogs—they weigh about 900 pounds—but it's still big. If you want to adopt a super-awesome pig like Bunwinkle, remember to do research and ask the breeder lots of questions Or even better, adopt from a piggy rescue.

Second, all dogs and pigs may not get along as well as Horace and Bunwinkle do. Dogs are hunters by nature and pigs get hunted, which means you may have problems if you put them together.

Not all dogs are proper and polite Boston Terriers like Horace.

Third, every kind of pet has specific needs, like diet and exercise. Make sure you know what those are before you adopt one.

P.S. While Shoo is awesome, not all raccoon are as friendly as he is. In fact, they can be kind of nasty, so it's best to leave them alone.

—PJ

Acknowledgments

Writing the Horace & Bunwinkle books is a blast! I'm able to enjoy it because of the wonderful people in my life who support me along the way.

My family is obviously a great help, so a huge thank you to Neil, CJ, Zach, and Jeff, plus the wonder pooches, Rosie and Rocky.

Professionally, I owe so much to my agent, Kari Sutherland, and my editor at Balzer + Bray, Kristin Rens, as well as the whole team at Harper-Collins. Thank you all for your continued support.

To Namina, Nan, and Celesta I share my undying gratitude. You three always know how to strengthen me.

I offer thanks to Divine Parents, who lift and guide me.

And lastly, I want to thank you, my dear readers, for following the adventures of this dynamic duo.